Sarah Gould

Poems

Sarah Gould

Poems

ISBN/EAN: 9783744653589

Printed in Europe, USA, Canada, Australia, Japan

Cover: Foto ©Andreas Hilbeck / pixelio.de

More available books at **www.hansebooks.com**

BY

SARAH GOULD.

"I love not less
Earth's loveliest bloom—wood-haunting lily-bells,
  Daisy or violet—for all loveliness
Of these I bring,—my fading Asphodels,
  Plucked on the hills of Immortality!
But, dear memorials of faint-pulsèd dreams,
Fields never sere, and amber-paven streams,
  And angels leaning from their opal sky
With your still dewy sweets,—
  I clasp you, though ye die!"

———————

NEW YORK:

RUDD & CARLETON, 130 GRAND ST.

(BROOKS BUILDING CORNER OF BROADWAY.)

M DCCC LX.

R. CRAIGHEAD,
Printer, Stereotyper, and Electrotyper.
Caxton Building,
81, 83, and 85 Centre Street.

CONTENTS.

ASPHODELS.

RESTORATION.

We grope through the dark,
  And shrink in dismay,
From the phantom-eyes stark,
  That glare on our way;

And we tremble, with fear,
  At our own spirit's tread,
Clinging fast to some dear
  Hope, withered and dead;

Which, nathless, would hold us
  In fealty still,
Ever seeking to fold us
  Firm bound to its will;

Then we catch the low tone
  Of a Voice that is clear;
And the distant Unknown
  Is a luminous Here,

Which kindles our feelings,
　And quickens our sight,
With glorious revealings
　Of beauty, and light,

And in that awaking,
　We feel the rebound
From our soul-leap in taking
　A measure profound

Of the chaos, inclosing
　Our innermost sense,
As Islands reposing
　'Mid ocean's Immense.

And, born into duty,
　We walk the new road,
Through labor to Beauty,
　Through Beauty to God;

The phantoms of terror
　Fall stricken, and stark,
And Truth pierces Error,
　Light pierces the Dark.

PROPHETIC GLIMPSES.

A LIGHT upon my spirit gleams,
  A light I rather feel than see;
It comes as come exalted dreams
  In hours of holiest ecstasy.

And deep within my inmost soul,
  While all my waiting senses kneel,
High glories to my view unroll,
  That language fails me to reveal.

A meaning strange and sweet I see
  In every thing, above, around,
Or in the haze of mystery,
  Or beings simple, or profound;

The music of the gurgling rill,
  By careless souls not understood;
The incense-cups the flowers fill
  With stories of the quiet wood;

In twilight's mellow distances,
  The momentary hush of noon,
In midnight's mute solemnities,
  And morn's exhilarating tune;

The pattering feet of dancing rain,
  Mysterious voices of the wind,
In the deep ocean's solemn strain,
  And deeper ocean of the mind.

As here thy spirit hand I hold,
  Thy fleshly robes are drawn away,
I see thy inner form unfold,
  From all the windings of its clay.

I see it scarred with wrong, and strife;
  Malice hath grazed it with her wand,
And the fell foes of truest life,
  In frowning aspect, round it stand.

Oh, heed them not, the senseless horde,
  Who track thee on thy lofty way,
Whose blackening thought, and act, and word,
  Would stain the very heart of day.

Oh, listen to the sound I hear!
  It comes, loud swelling, once again,
And breaks upon my ravished ear,
  A conquering, a victorious strain!

Mark the high triumph of the song,
  Now borne so sweetly on the gale;
Ah. never more can False, and Wrong,
  Over the True, and Right, prevail.

Then calmly front the cloud, and storm,
   And work thy work with patient will,
Faith, Hope, and Love, thy heart shall warm,
   And their own prophecies fulfill.

THE TWIN ANGELS.

On, a little blue-eyed angel
   Bending from the calm serene,
Seems she like a sweet Evangel,
   With her gentle look and mien.

Flaxen are her flowing tresses,
   Silvery in the sheeny light,
Not an angel looks, but blesses
   This young seraph, heavenly bright.

There's another bud of sweetness
   Hanging just above us now,
Oh, how rich in their completeness
   Are her radiant cheek and brow!

Ringlets ebon black, and glossy,
   Fall her slender waist below,
As a gauzy mantle flossy,
   Waving ever to and fro.

And her eyes flash vibratory
　　Blackness, like a midnight storm,
Yet pervaded by a glory
　　That irradiates her form.

Arms of form they are entwining
　　Laughing as if full of glee;
And I inly muse, divining
　　Who this younger one may be.

Lo, she bends to me with kisses
　　From those lips of ruddy hue;
They're our darling little Lizzie's,
　　Sweet as morning with its dew.

Oh, the rapture of their singing!
　　I can almost catch the rhyme,
All the while their white arms flinging
　　Here and there, in keeping time.

Weaving, now, the gayest dances
　　With the countless cherubs there;
In their whirls it often chances
　　Lizzie's ringlets frolic where

Lydia's silken locks are flowing,—
　　As a cloudlet, pearly white,
Where the twilight shades are growing
　　Still retains the sun's soft light.

Thus, in all their infant features,
 Married differences shine,
But so perfect are their natures,
 So entirely intertwine,

In a graceful harmonizing,
 That their blended spirits seem
As two stars, that, in their rising,
 Twinkle with the self-same gleam.

THE SERPENT HORROR.

Because we have wandered in error,
 The serpent is armed with a sting;
And wisdom is clad in the symbols of terror,
 Our souls to their centre to bring.   E. D. H.

I WITH pain had wrestled fiercely,
 Void of slumber, through the night,
When there came a dream to pierce me
 Through and through, with wild affright.

I was walking in a forest,
 In the damp, autumnal year,
Where the frost, with touch the sorest,
 Crisped the leaves up brown and sere;

When, upon a little hillock
   Blooming 'mid the dearth around,
Underneath a high and still rock,
   I a little violet found.
And it nodded, O, so quaintly!
   As I bent above its bloom,
Though it seemed to cling more faintly
   To the strength of its perfume.

And I whispered, "Wherefore hiding
   Thus away from mortal view?"
Oh its glance was so confiding
   From its modest eye of blue,
As its golden-crested finger
   It extended up to me,
Saying slowly, "I would linger
   Still a little in the lea;
While the frost is whitely roving
   Till the rosy light of morn,
I would nestle soft and loving
   Till another bud was born.

There are blooms more proud and stately
   Which in haughty grandeur grow,
On the hill-side towering greatly,
   'Mid the sunset's crimson glow;

There are vines that drape your arbors
　　With a gold and purple hue,
While this quiet nook still harbors
　　The pale violet's tender blue.

In this loved and lovely dwelling,
　　This so deeply sheltered nook,
My sweet voice would still be telling
　　Of the hymnings in the brook
Round about us, morn and even,
　　From kind nature's ministries,
Ever giving and receiving
　　Fraternizing sympathies."

I was listening to the flower
　　To its soft voice sweet and low,
When with fascinating power
　　A bright serpent glided slow,
From a crevice, and around me
　　Flickered with a graceful sweep,
And I stirred not, for it bound me
　　In the subtle cords of sleep.

It approached me nearer, nearer,
　　With its glossy, glittering coils,
And I saw it clearer, clearer,
　　Powerless to escape its toils!

For I could not, from my sleeping,
    Summon strength enough to start,
When as lightning swiftly leaping,
    It fell writhing on my heart.

And I felt it twining, twining,
    With its circlets icy cold,
And I saw the shining, shining
    Of each tight'ning, clinging fold;
Till with nerve and fibre shrinking
    From the rigor of its grasp,
In its fierce embraces sinking,
    Faint and fainter grew each grasp.

Seemed the firmament as falling
    In dense blackness to the ground,
And a shadow, most appalling,
    Settled upon all around!
Still more tightly did he fold me!
    Tightly and more tightly still!
And I had not strength to hold me
    In resistance to his will;
Then with terror inly quivering,
    Of its poisonous breath I drank,
And it sent a fatal shivering
    Through me, as in death I sank.

Was it death ? nay, 't was not dying,
But a sinking, soaring, flying,
And the furies seemed to goad me,
Memories of the past, to load me
With the dark and scentless flowers
Which had sprung in noxious bowers,
Where, through all the lingering hours,
Drizzled dank and poisonous showers;
In each blossom, folded close,
Was a serpent's dark repose,
And instead of perfumed kisses
You but caught a serpent's hisses!

Even the trees, around me there,
Tall and scaly serpents were,
Every branch a snaky form,
Writhing, hissing in the storm!
Earth, on which I feared to tread,
Seemed a monster, dark and dread,
Brooks and rivers, and the ocean,
Took a twining, slimy motion;
Ay, the clouds above them all,
Changed to serpents, great and small.
"Oh, ye heavens!" I shuddering moan,
"I too am a serpent grown.
Hissing, twining, coiling, rattling,
With the hideous serpents battling

I sink beneath their loathsome breath,
Father, Father, give me death!"

To die, to die! it may not be;
There is no peace but victory;
Then patiently abide the strife,
There is no death but only Life!

THE CONSECRATION.

A HAND was laid upon my brow,
A chilling shudder trembled through;
    And, down my inmost soul,
A voiceful silence seemed to creep;
My trance became more fixed and deep,
    Beneath its strong control.

"Behold!" it said; I looked, and lo
Whole armies, marching to and fro,
    Before my startled eyes;
I heard the terrifying crash,
The cannon's roar, the stunning clash,
    That rent the shuddering skies!

I saw the desolating crush,
The hopeless, the despairing rush

Of souls, by terror racked;
The want, and woe, and cankering care,
Ruin and death, that every where,
   By tears, and blood, were tracked!

This horror passed; and lo, I stood
Within a dark and gloomy wood.
   "Behold!" my Leader saith.
I looked, but sickened, turned away;
For there a murdered traveller lay,
   Wrestling alone with death!

Onward we journeyed, coming where
Loud shouts, and laughter, filled the air,
   And thoughtless thousands flocked;
A gallows lifted to the sky,
God's image in humanity,
   That winds, irreverent, rocked!

Oh, murder's self had not the power,—
Nor all the evil battles shower
   Along their blood-stained sod,—
To match this agonizing sight,
Done in the name of Law and Right,
   Done in the name of God!

Still on we went, and reached, at length,
A city, glorious in strength,

The pride of all the earth;
But even a fiend would blush to name
The wrong and woe, the crime and shame,
    That in its heart had birth!

There man, his brother man betrayed,
Hatred, distrust, and envy, made
    Within its walls, their nest;
Lust, avarice, pride, and dark deceit,
Seemed with each other to compete,
    In every human breast.

Religion! over me there falls
A dark'ning shadow, like a pall's,
    As of her shame I speak!
From all her churches rang no Law,
The weak to cheer, the bad to awe,
    She was so shorn and weak!

Thither the purse-proud worshipper,
And his sleek priest, with silken stir,
    Came, every Sabbath day,
Together, in each stately hall,
On God, in hollow words, to call,
    And publicly to pray.

No entrance for the humble poor!
None but the rich find open door;

Jesus himself might wait!
Wan memory shudders to reveal
The records which their hearts conceal,
  Of Pomp's delusive state.

Sadly I turned to look on one
Whose face was radiant as a sun;
  "And is there then, no cure?
Nothing but wickedness?" I cried,
" Whereby the Good is crucified;
  And must it thus endure?"

"Yes! till, with tongues of living flame,
God's ministers this truth proclaim,—
  'Love is the life of good,
The only medicine we can give
Is, teaching men the art to live
  In human brotherhood.' "

HEART-RICH.

THY love, how rich in its excess,
  How fervent, and how manifold;
Thy overflowing tenderness,
  And sympathetic wealth untold!

Blest spirits from the higher sphere
   Bend lovingly, thy pathway o'er;
Angels of beauty linger near,
   Their blessings on thy head to pour.

Think what a privilege it is,
   A life so roseate as thine,
A treasury of sweetest bliss,
   The largess of a love divine.

I count thy treasures, so replete
   With all that could delight, or bless,
And, lady! I can but repeat,
   Thy life should be a blessedness!

In all thy lineaments I trace
   A gentle nature, undefiled
By the rude storms, that oft efface
   The attributes of Love's own child.

Then, in thy very sweetness strong,
   Securely may thy soul rejoice,
And living gladness swell the song
   To which thy spirit finds a voice.

APRIL.

My thoughts are wandering in the woods to-
    day,
  Over green carpets of the velvet moss,
  While overhead wierd branches intercross
The purple heavens, whose fleecy mist-wreaths
    play
With answering mist-wreaths, shadowed on the
    ground,
  Creeping, as wavelets o'er a slumbering sea,
  Or white drifts sliding from stern winter's
    knee
By the sun's glory Chrism'd! I have found
  The Arbutus, pink with promises of spring;
  The Wind flower and the Violet, still cling
  To the sweet shelter of their winter home,
  Nestled 'mid tangled roots and fragrant loam ;
For Notus tempts not with alluring breath
The timid buds that Eurus dooms to death.

SUNSET.

Day is fading, a strange sadness
   Darkens down within my breast;
Like the shadow of some gladness
   Slowly sinking to its rest.

Ay, the sun is setting, setting;
   And there gleams no evening star,—
Will a night of dark forgetting
   All these mingled memories mar?

No, not e'en in blissful sleeping
   Shall they sink to brief repose;
Till the angels in their keeping
   Fold the precious treasures close.

And the promise of to-morrow,
   Sweet assurance, bright as brief,
Gilds the darkness of my sorrow,
   Lifts the curtain of my grief.

Promise oft so lightly spoken,
   It but a dim mockery seems,
Still, it's bread that's blessed and broken
   By the Angels of our dreams.

THE VIOLET.

A VIOLET, buried in deep woods, am I,
  Quietly nestled in my solitude,
  Loving the voices of the true and good;
With petals open to the kindly sky,
I drink the glimpsing light, the twinkling dew,
  Shed from the Father's ever-bounteous hand,
  Who looks upon me with a smile, so bland
It fills my vailéd heart with odors new.
Not for the world's applauses would I grow
  In any spot less hallowed by His love,
Though gaudier grandeur round my home might
      glow,
  And flowers, more beauteous, proudly nod
      above;
No! the green darkness of my dell is dear
For the Great Love that clings so warmly round
  me here.

AN ECSTASY.

OH! strike the mute lyre!
Awake its full fire
    Once again;

Pour forth all around,
That musical sound,
   That sweet strain.

With the last tone's receding,
Bright angels were speeding,
   Full of love,
With their pinions spread, fair,
On the jubilant air,
   Far above.

I can count them! ah, no!
For so swiftly they go
   Trooping by,
Their pearly wings beaming
As fitfully gleaming
   They fly.

Breathe softly that strain!
They are coming again,
   See ye not?
Softer yet! they will hear;
They are near, very near
   To this spot.

Ah! no more I behold,
For I shiver with cold,
   And ice-chill

Are the drops on my brow,
And my blood, in its flow,
Becomes still !

MOSS-MUSIC.

Now radiant joy sits smiling in my breast,—
  These fragrant pinks and pansies fair, fresh
    culled,
Wood Violets and Mosses, lately lulled
In shady nooks, by rippling brooks, to rest;
With the rich grandeur of each mossy crest
  So green and moist, the blossoms seem to vie
  With their bright hues, as lovingly they lie,
Dizzy from their own perfumes, unconfest,
Green mosses from the brookside, mosses sweet!
  Say, have ye heard the singing of the Wren,
  The Thrush, or Blackbird, by your brooks ?
    oh, then:
I pray you, if you can, some strain repeat:
Bend closer still, bright mosses; now I hear,
A bird like music, sylvan-sweet and clear.

TO ———

Thou heart of hearts! pure, gentle, and benign,
Strengthen, improve, inspire, this heart of mine,
As the dull earth the sunbeams penetrate,
These brilliant rays my spirit permeāte;
And clear, along its vailéd way, I trace
The high unfoldings of the Infinite Grace,
In thy unfettered, and far-reaching mind,
Prophet, and Priest, and Lover of thy kind!

O, I could bow in silence, and revere
One scarcely fettered to this mortal sphere,
Such inward glory sits upon thy brow,
And, from thy lips, such heavenly teachings
    flow,
Timid with awe at first, I feared to roam
The exalted sphere which forms thy spirit's
    home.

Though strength, and greatness, on thy steps
    attend,
The gentler virtues with their rigors blend
Sweet Love and Wisdom, in thy spirit mild,
And unassuming as a little child,

Simple and truthful, earnest and sincere,
We can but love thee, whom we so revere.

Though all around, as waiting thy command,
With brows severe, the souls of Wisdom stand,
Seraphs of Love on wings irradiant fly,
Flashing athwart the clearness of thy sky,
In dazzling gleams of such immortal light,
My eyelids droop to shield my trancéd sight.

And now, methinks, more vast the arches grow;
Oh God! what see I, passing to and fro?
Beings perfected so beyond compare,
Filling with brightness all the ravished air,
To the wide hum of such entrancing strains,
The languid blood seems sleeping in my veins!

This deep excess of sweetness pours around
A cloud of glory, and a flood of sound,
Of such melodious, and pervading power,
My soul grows richer from this very hour
With a more noble sense of high and true,
More lovely love, and beauty's fairer hue.
This blessed vision shall return, in gleams,
Dazzling but soft, to all my golden dreams.
And spite of sorrow, pain, and inward strife,
Wreathe a bright halo round my future life.

O, gentle spirit! whose serene control
Moves to exalt and purify my soul;
Whose inspirations, hopeful and sublime,
Shall work their purpose to remotest time,
It is more blest to give, than to receive,
Mildest of Mentors, well may I believe,
The rapturous joys, that on my soul attend,
This hour, on thee, in deeper streams descend.

O yes, I see, but never may impart,
How beats thy heart with the Eternal Heart!
How soul to soul, and mind to mastering mind,
Thy thoughts, in God, their sphering centre find;
How His high glories, with too rich excess,
In hearts like thine their vailéd beams express,
Humanely vailed to spare our feebleness;
While the fair temple, now thy soul's abode,
Glows with the presence of the living God.

TEMPEST-TOSSED.

When the wild, wild winds awake from sleep,
And over the earth in fury sweep,
From angry sky to heaving deep,
          Come terror and dismay.

Changing for ever, from quick to slow,
Fearfully loud, or strangely low,
They fill us with awe, as on they go,
    Enveloped in mystery.

When the dread storm-spirit sends them forth,
From the far, far regions of the north,
Earth tremblingly shrinks as if most loth
    To encounter their array.

They hurry along, and laugh, to mock
The quivering trees, which seem to flock
Closely together, and wait the shock
    Of the terrible affray!

The proudest ash, and the mighty oak,
Are shorn of strength by their sturdy stroke,
And their giant limbs are wrenched and broke,
    And in scattered fragments lie.

And feebler ones, that had fondly made
Their humble homes in its spreading shade,
Nor felt, in its sheltering arms, afraid,—
    Their shivered honors fly!

As helpless, oh timid soul, art thou,
And wilt need some sheltering oak, I trow,
When the storms of life shall fiercely blow,
    In hurricanes on thee.

Look up! look up, to the blest abode!
Lean on the arm of thy Saviour God,
Confidingly, as thou walk'st life's road;
   For thy sheltering guide, is He.

Oh yes! but the tension of mind will tire,
In this upward gaze, and thy soul desire
One like itself, though it were higher,
   Its Guardian to be.

Ah, ever may friendship over me fling
The shielding cloak of its sheltering wing;
A faithful friend is a precious thing,
   And a sacred one to me.

The sweetest thought to my spirit given
Of our final home in the halls of heaven,
Is this, that the ties will ne'er be riven,
   Of friends in Eternity.

OUR VALLEY LILY.

A pale and modest flow'ret is in our gardens
    found,
So close to earth, it has its birth, it would be
    seldom seen,
But for the heavenly fragrance, it scattereth
    around,
A choice perfume, that makes the bloom as
    regal as a Queen.

And gentle human Spirits are growing thus on
    earth,
Who shrink away, as if the day their native
    heaven shut out,
The incense of whose spirit-life betrays their
    heavenly birth,
By the pure and hallowed perfume, their pre-
    sence breathes about.

Far from their holy influence the vile and erring
    flee,
So sweet and fair, in cloistral air, the home
    which they inherit,
The purely chaste and glorified, a blissful com-
    pany,
Seek evermore the chancel door, and love to
    linger near it.

Thus Alice, gentle Alice, thy meeknesses serene,
A halo shed around thy head, which crowns
   thee as a Queen.

CANZONETTA.

TO LITTLE FLOY.

LEAF, and bud, and blossom,
   As ye spring to birth,
On the bounteous bosom
   Of our mother earth,
Ye dispel all sadness,
   Put to flight all care,
Make delight, and gladness,
   Leap up everywhere!

Dreary! Oh, how dreary!
   Were this world of ours,
And how sad and weary,
   But for gentle flowers.
What a dismal glooming,
   Darkens every scene
Where no flowers are blooming,
   Where no leaves are green.

Floy! within thy bosom,
　Waiting thy command,
Are leaf, bud, and blossom
　Ready to expand.
Thou their growth must cherish,
　Nurture their perfume,
Or will droop, and perish,
　Leaf, and bud, and bloom.

When thou shalt array them,
　Beautiful and bright,
Angels shall convey them
　To the realms of light.
There to bloom for ever
　In celestial bowers,
Where no winter ever
　Blights the precious flowers.

THE LOVE CIRCLE.

Never taken for another
Could he be, thy peerless brother,
Radiant as eastern skies
With the chrism of sunrise,
As, in loving-kindness, he
Bends a Christ-look over thee.

4

List! oh, listen! he is seeking,
With a musical, low, speaking,
Both our spirits to impress
With the sweetest tenderness;
More inspiring me, the while,
With the sunlight of his smile.

Vibratory nerves, be still!
Hush thy waywardness, my will!
Pulses, yet more noiseless beat,
And, as in the heart you meet,
Let no sudden thrill declare
All the rapture trembling there.

Oh, what transports thrill my frame!
As a glory-kindling flame,
These divine revealings flow,
Permeating, through and through,
All my inmost depths of being,
Till my life seems fleeing, fleeing.

Hark! he says, or seems to say,
" Would'st thou heavenly realms survey,
Leave thy home, and soar with me,
Not with fear, but trustingly;
Leave the earth and its hopes below
The soul alone treads the path we go."

For a moment I waver to and fro
As a bird will swing on a swaying bough,
Then upward, as swift as the rushing storm,
I am borne, as I cling to his perfect form;
On, and on, over fields of ether,
Through limitless realms we soar together!

And now in the midst of a glorious band,
In the midst of a glorious scene, I stand;
His circle above, is a Circle of Love;
In the smile of the Father they live, and move;
Through my inmost nature its glow I feel,
As, with reverent love, at His feet I kneel.

"Father! dear Father!" I joyfully cry,
And my voice is echoed along the sky;
As the sweet appeal to my lip is springing,
From angel tongues is an anthem ringing,
And I join in the chorus, "Oh, Father dear!"
My loving soul draws softly near.

Now on my forehead rests, gently caressing,
A nail-scarred hand overfull of blessing.
And, "Daughter beloved," He saith, "arise!"
As with tearful eyes, in a glad surprise,
I feel the blessing, a holy presence,
Thrill my soul to its ultimate essence.

I turn to the beautiful spirit bands,
Where my radiant guardian angel stands,
With his glittering wings but half out-spreaa;
And a halo of glory around his head,
That, over his flowing curls of brown,
Sheds a threefold lustre, a triple crown.

Brightest, he seems, of the brilliant throng,
And as now, with wide wings waved along,
They are onward borne 'mid the amber clouds,
Oh, God! how each flashing pinion crowds
With crimson glories my reeling brain,
Till my eyelids droop with their weight of pain!

Right hither their rapid way they wing,
O holy Christ! what a song they sing!
Such sounds have never my spirit stirred;
Oh list; for methinks, I can catch some word,—
"Love! Love!" is the chorus, and Love the
    theme;
Oh, can this be but a fleeting dream!

A golden harp they've brought to me,
I touch its strings in an ecstasy,
And gushing song from my soul is leaping,
And wings start out from my shoulders sweeping.
O wonder, I feel their plumes unfold
In waves of purple and gleams of gold.

Oh glorious wings! will ye bear me on
Where the angel band in their flight have gone?
They pause, they hover for me, they stay;
They beckon, they beckon to call me away;
I fly, I fly, like a bird; I am winging
Up, up through the light, 'mid the perfumes
    singing.

A moment, a moment, blest vision of light,
Let me know ere I go if I see thee aright.
Afar the old earth as a vapor I see
Where the friends I have left are watching for
    me;
The choir of the angels grows dim, and more dim,
The fairest fades last, till I lose even him.

RECOGNITION.

I SEE thee walking, hand in hand, with Fame:
I hear the throbbings of the loud acclaim
Of souls, who, at the tremblings of thy lyre
Catch inspiration from its chords of fire;
Whilst thou, in regnant beauty, as a queen,
Rul'st in all hearts, with dignity serene.

Oh, could my song give language to my heart,
What answering music from thy own would
     start!
But my untutored tongue is poor, and weak,
The silent victories of thy soul to speak,
Or yet some prayer, in deep'ning love, to pour
That God may keep, and bless thee, evermore!

LIGHT IN DARKNESS.

Ah, hast thou borne the load of care,
    That weighs the spirit down?
Drank the black waters of despair,
    Thy every hope that drown?

Seen all the stars of joy go out,
    As, one by one, they sank
Into the soundless sea of doubt,
    Leaving thy heavens a blank?

Felt, as a flame, the darkness burn
    Into thy fainting heart,
And could nor sun, nor moon discern,
    Their healing to impart?

Felt darksome doubts, and nameless fears,
　　Crowding upon thy brain,
While the deep fount of mellowing tears
　　Withheld refreshing rain?

Felt in thy soul as desolate,
　　Unfriended, and alone,
As chained, by some relentless fate,
　　To the Promethean stone?

Ah, yes! the vulture's beak I see ·
　　Smite on thy spirit form,
And the swift hail of agony,
　　And sorrow's whelming storm!

Thy cherished hope, and love, and pride,
　　Like reeds are cloven down;
While doubt and dark despair, allied,
　　In clouds of horror frown.

Still I feel a painful wonder
　　That a spirit, formed as thine,
Had not trod its trials under,
　　With a potency divine.

He, thy loved one, early sinking
　　In the frost of wint'ry skies,
That bright one, so early drinking
　　The new wines of Paradise!

Now a radiant angel, roving
   In a sphere of perfect bliss,—
Would'st thou he were longer proving
   The heart-wasting cares of this?

No, thou readest not so dimly
   Of the Future, of the Now;
While new trust, and love, supremely
   Rest upon thy spirit brow,

The serene inspiring glances,
   Beaming from his heavenly eye;
Every feeling it entrances
   To a sweet intensity.

With a pure, exalted mission,
   Pallid suffering comes to thee;
Let it speak the full expression
   Of its destined ministry.

Oh, behold! he stands before us,
   Dazzling to our mental sight,
As his presence kindles o'er us
   Flashes of bewildering light;

Of a sunshine, radiating
   All my inmost spirit through;
Of a love-fire, consecrating
   With a baptism pure and true.

Oh! I bless thee, noble spirit,
   For the vision thou hast given;
Through its presence we inherit
   Yet another hold on heaven.

In my soul comes such a longing
   To untwine this fleshly coil,
So to join the spirits, thronging
   On the Paradisean soil!—

Yet it is not well to cherish
   Such intensity of fire;
So, with the sweet vision, perish
   All this over-wrought desire!

All the past, with peace, surrender;
   Crown the present with new joy;
And thy latest pang shall render,
   To thy arms, thy darling Boy!

THE LIFTED VAIL.

Oh, Lady! lift thy mournful eyes;
   Why should despair so blind their sight?
See! yonder in the red'ning skies,
   Wrestles the all-controlling light.

Angels, to minister relief,
  Are bending from the calm above;
Oh, fleetly, may this chilling grief
  Yield to the influence of their love.

Dear Lady, very well I know
  Thy inner life is clouded o'er
With a benumbing, deadening woe,
  A clinging mist on sea and shore;
Though from thy suffering heart will fall
  The mellow notes of hope and cheer,
And thy pale hand would lift the pall
  That darkens o'er the stricken, here.

A heavenly prophecy I bear,
  Of Peace, upon my spirit lips,
Thou canst discern the ocean where
  Its polished wings, that halcyon dips.
It comes to teach that strength divine
  Shall triumph o'er this martyrdom,
And that high victory shall be thine,
  Which but to struggling souls can come.

Already hath the darkness flung
  Apart her mantle, torn and gray,
And, though the dawn hath feebly sprung,
  'T will culminate to perfect day.

Be patient then, for, bravely borne,
  Shall Triumph on thy banners rest,
And the dark demon hence be torn,
  That clings, a nightmare, to thy breast.

Divinest joys my spirit fill
  While thus I pierce the darkness through,
And see thy future clear, and still,
  And beautiful, as heaven's own blue.
As thy dissolving gloom I scan,
  With a most earnest spirit glance,
The wings of warder angels fan
  My cheek, and deeper grows the trance.

A spirit form is near us now,
  Of manly presence, proud and bold,
The language of his ample brow
  Is full of histories untold.
He draws thee to his heart of hearts,
  His arms around thee gently twine,
And the delicious strain imparts
  To thee, a prescience Divine.

No longer weak, thou standest up,
  With heart redeemed from loss, and doubt;
Thou drinkest of the mingled cup
  The angel of thy life pours out.

Strength, born of weakness, shall be thine,
    Hope, from the anguish of despair,
The faith, and power, of love divine,
    Shall all the erring past repair.

TO ———

I LOVE thee, lady! and have loved thee long;
And every utterance of thy simplest song
Finds, in my soul, an echo warm and true,
And clearly opens, to my mental view,
Thy spirit's quiet and exalted home,
Whither good angels love so well to come,
And often, lady, from the realms of thought,
A votive offering I to thee have brought,
But when, all trembling, I approached the shrine
Where burned a fire so lofty and divine,
I feared my gift too simple was to place
Beside the first-fruits which that altar grace,
And I have turned, reluctantly, away,
With loitering steps, unwilling to obey.

But now I view thee as a sister soul,
And journey with thee to the self-same goal,
I feel new life through all my pulses start,
While thus I read the pages of thy heart,

Rarely to mortals, in this nether sphere,
Come revelations so exceeding clear.
Thy spirit's features I as plainly trace
As, in a mirror, my reflected face.
Would that my soul might be unvailéd thus,
That my flesh garments were as luminous!

One moment more, dear lady, I intrude;
Oh, deem me not presumptuous, vain, or rude;
Unskilled, unlettered, is this heart of mine,
Simple and childish, when compared with thine;
Yet see! this harp, which is at my command,
Was strung and given me by an angel's hand,
Who taught me all the beatific skill,
To wake its numbers whensoe'er I will;
And listen, lady! as, that skill to prove,
Across the silken strings my fingers move.
Oh, hearest thou the rapturous tones that flow
From its ethereal chords! while on heaven's
    brow
The angels listen, or, with waving wing,
Send back, responsive, the sweet songs they
    sing!
Their choral theme, transcendently sublime,
Is the ascending, glorious march of time,
Whose mingling numbers rise, and fall, and
    swell,
Like the high pealings of a minster bell.
5

Would we more perfect and harmonious grow,
Thought, word, and action, thus should interflow,
Keeping full concord, and symphonious time,
With heaven, and earth, and ocean's mystic
    chime.

"QUEEN HELEN."

THEY who profess the floral tongues to know,
    Say that each blossom hath one, all its own,
That from the lips of this, for ever flow
    The prophecies of change; that in its tone
There lurks a sadness, such as loved ones feel
    When those who loved them have become
    estranged.
But these fair leaves no waning faith conceal,
    They bear the language of a heart unchanged
To thee, Queen Helen! from my golden bowers;
    Full of the memories of the treasured past,
These crimson leaflets of bignonia flowers
    Trembling with rapture, at thy feet I cast,
Thou canst discern the deeper sense, that lies
Wreathed in their heart, unseen of unanointed
    eyes.

CROSS AND CROWN.

DEEP within thy inmost spirit,
   Where the herds of rough, and rude,
Cannot drink, nor browse anear it,—
   Far from all that would intrude,

Lies a waveless, sunny, lakelet,
   So serenely crystalline,
Earthly voices cannot wake it
   From its silences divine.

Birds of brightest hues are winging
   O'er its bosom hushed, and still,
While the raptures of their singing
   Its profoundest waters thrill.

Earnest hopes, and sportive wishes,
   Round in circling eddies turn;
Playful fancies, like bright fishes,
   Glitter in the Naiad's urn.

When discordant tones, or voices,
   From the outward, to thee come,
Undisturbed, thy soul rejoices
   In this quiet spirit-home.

God is ever very tender
  Of a soul incased like thine,
In a frame so frail and slender;
  And our angel-friends incline,

Evermore, to shield, and cherish,
  One whose life must pine, and wait,—
Leaving no sweet hope to perish
  Under a relentless fate.

Suffering is a purifier,
  If we will not shrink, and make
More intense the scathing fire
  By vain strugglings at the stake.

What if, for life's little hour,
  Fleshly chains are round us thrown?
See we not, it is the power
  By which martyrs win their crown?

Ruder souls would bear, unfeeling,
  Shocks that stun thy every sense;
Standing firm, while thou wert reeling
  With an agony intense.

Still in musing, as I ponder
  O'er life's deeply hidden things,
Evermore there comes the wonder,
  Whence are its exhaustless springs?

Whence the latent strength, upspringing
  In such gentle, timid souls?
A bright halo o'er them flinging,
  Which, before our eyes, unrolls

The sublime, and startling, histories
  Of their unseen, inner life,
Deep revealings, deeper mysteries,
  With untold experience rife?

And One answers, in a murmur
  Of subdued delight, and saith,
Clay may fail, but souls grow firmer,
  By their inbred Love and Faith;
Clay may die, but souls grow firmer,
  Soaring, victors over death!

THE RIVULET.

A LITTLE stream went flowing,
  And humming, towards the sea,
With valley lilies growing
  Beside it, tenderly.

Tall trees, their arms above it
　With sheltering kindness spread;
Well did the Sunbeams love it
　And laugh along its bed.

The earth unvailed her bosom
　That she might shield its flow,
And bending bud and blossom
　Reflect themselves below.
The still and solemn midnight
　Its holy influence lent;
With the sacred moon's half-hid light,
　And whispering star beams blent.

All heavenly visitations,
　To gladden the sweet stream,—
All misty exhalations,
　Were mingled with its dream.
The silent darkness doubled,
　Just ere the morning broke,
Its seeming depth, untroubled,
　Till a breezy laughter woke.

The twilight oft would linger,
　Entranced, above it long,
As a maid, with lifted finger,
　Stands listening to a song.

The plants and tree-roots twining,
  Through the earth all parched with thirst,
Would drink till their berries shining
  And beautiful globes, would burst.

No poisonous leaf or blossom,
  Distained its tranquil flow,
Though on its lovely bosom
  They floated, to and fro,
And because it ever went gliding
  Round rock, and crag, and hill,
Some said 't was faithless, biding
  No certain course, or will.

Its motions were so noiseless,
  The bubbles, as they broke
On the pebbly brink, leapt voiceless;
  Not an Echo-nymph awoke,
Till its crystal cascades, bounding,
  Went down the hills with a leap,
A glorious music sounding
  Till the Naiads sprang from sleep.
And then, with a trancéd motion,
  An even step, and true,
Life's flowery vale, to the ocean,
  It danced and rippled through.

IRENE.

BEAUTIFUL, tender,
　　And gentle IRENE?
Oh, wilt thou surrender,
　　With spirit serene,
A life, bright and vernal,
　　In freshness of youth,
For riches eternal,
　　Of goodness and truth?
Wilt thou bow thy sweet head
　　At the summoning voice
Of Him who hath said,
　　"Come to me and rejoice!
When sorrows attend thee,
　　In sickness or woe,
For I will befriend thee,
　　And lead thee to know
That Peace which, descending,
　　Flows on like a river,
So blending, unending,
　　Sweet harmonies, ever."

Though whirlwinds are raging,
　　And rude tempests sweep,
And the elements waging
　　Wild war on the deep,

His Infinite Will
　All their fury can stay,
His low " Peace be still !"
　They forever obey.

Then, calm with assurance,
　Repose on His breast;
Be strong in endurance ;
　He giveth thee rest.
His angels He sendeth
　On thee to attend ;
Above thee He bendeth,
　A father, and friend.
In each trial hour,
　As a radiant zone,
His right arm of power
　Around thee is thrown.

A Saviour, now wearing
　His Infinite charms,
As a lambkin, is bearing
　Thy soul in His arms;
Or, borne on His bosom,
　To regions above,
Thou shalt be as a blossom
　Of goodness and love,

In His garden of beauty
  Forever to bloom,
In the green strength of duty,
  And love's own perfume.

We will not forget thee
  Our darling IRENE,
But, star-jeweled, set thee
  As light of each scene;
Thy love will bloom sweetly,
  Thy memory be green,
Till, deathless, we meet thee,
  Our darling IRENE!

HEAVENLY PEACE.

On light, intensely golden,
  Yet mellow in its hue,
How softly it is molten
  In the empyrean blue!

Oh, spirits bright, I hail ye!
  Companions of my way,
No danger can assail me,
  Where'er my footsteps stray.

Oh, angels! most entrancing,
　Are your supernal charms,
As, lovingly advancing,
　Ye wave your snowy arms.

Oh, white wings, gently smoothing
　My lips, and cheek, and brow,
Serenely ye are soothing
　My wildest fancies now!

Oh, mother, queen of Heaven,
　Thy smiles upon me rest;
Once more to me is given
　To slumber on thy breast.

Oh, slumber most alluring,
　All heavenly and divine
Oh, peace for aye enduring,
　Joy! Joy! that it is mine.

THE FLOWER BASKET.

A BASKET of flowers—the basket of moss—
A braid of green rushes, thrown lightly across
The frolicsome blooms, which peep from between
A fringe of bright laurel leaves, shining and
　　green;

The crimson verbena, the cottager's child,
With pinks, single pinks, by no culture defiled,
Sad widows in mourning, and bachelors true,
In dresses of white, pink, purple and blue;
Facetious old bachelors! taking a nap,
With heads pillowed soft, in the flower spirit's
　　lap,
While pansies, geraniums, and sweet scented
　　blooms,
Beguile the swift hours with songs and per-
　　fumes;
A vision of beauty, which gladdens my view,
As the flowers are gladdened by sunlight and
　　dew

THE DARK RIVER.

ONCE, over my sleeping,
　This vision came sweeping:
I wandered alone by a deep river's side:
　　Their white arms entwining,
　　The Naiads, reclining
Floated down with the crystalline tide.

　　O'er the bright waters bending,
　　The wood Nymphs were blending

Their long shining tresses, that flowingly swept
 The wavelets' soft bosom,
 Where leaflet and blossom
Were rocked to and fro, as they slept.

 And here as I strayed,
 With heart all dismayed
By the sorrows that came in a throng,
 A Nymph, with a face
 Full of sweetness and grace,
Sat singing an exquisite song.

 And as I drew near,
 Stooping forward to hear
Her low and melodious singing,
 She raised her soft eyes,
 Full of pleasant surprise,
And her voice, o'er the bright waters ring-
  ing,

 Stirred the pleasant profound,
 The air trembled around,
Her jubilant music rose higher,
 Till my rapturous brain
 Thrilled with consummate pain,
And kindled my senses with fire.

Then I shrank from the cold
Of her tightening hold,
And we sank with a moan and a shiver;
My soul shudders now,
And damp is my brow,
As I think of that dark flowing river

We plunged with the speed
Of a rushing storm steed
Through the depths of that whirling abyss,
And the cold as a dart,
Sent a pang through my heart,
Yet it thrilled with a transport of bliss.

Above and below,
The stars, to and fro,
As sentinels moved o'er the stream;
But their wavering light
On the ripples fell bright,
In spirals of silvery gleam.

With merriest glances,
And gracefulest dances,
Fair forms, wheeled around on the tide,
"Oh give *me* a lyre,
Sweet soul! and inspire
Such joy in my bosom," I cried.

Suddenly I seemed uplifted,
In their mazes slowly drifted,
Amid melodies ecstatic;
And the lyre my touch obeying,
I, with them, was sweetly playing
Symphonies and airs erratic.

And my lips, too, were unsealed,
And to me there were revealed
Canticles of Love Divine;
And I chanted one sweet strain
O'er and o'er, and o'er again,
Ever, thus, to make it mine.

But their songs were for my sleep,
As they trembled through the deep,
Though the vision's light will stay,
And the memory of the singing
Will my soul revisit, bringing
Bright and holy thoughts, alway.

O, the rapture of my waking
From that slumber! day was breaking,
And the heavens were all aglow;
Light upon the eastern skies
Flashed as heavenly prophecies,
And a voice distinctly low,

Whispered to my spirit-ear,
"Be of good and sunny cheer;
Let thy cares and sorrows cease,
Though life's waters, deep and cold,
Darkly over thee have rolled,
Brief is their ungentle power,
And within thy soul, this hour,
Angels sing of love and peace."

THE BRIGHT RIVER.

WHAT discordances chaotic
Still dispute with us the way;
How the senses rule, despotic,
Bearing the soul's life away;
While all false and baseless Fay-dreams
Creep like truths into the heart,
Banishing the fairest day-beams
That would purer light impart.

Thus the homes which we inherit,—
Beautiful beyond compare,—
Harbor, each, a crouching spirit,
All too weak to will, or dare!

And our eyes we're ever closing
  To the light, so freely given,
'Mid inglorious joys reposing,
  All unmindful of our Heaven,
And the angels hovering o'er us,
  Beckoning us, so kindly, on—
Blessed spirits, who, before us,
  To the blissful realms have gone.

Oh, my sisters! oh, my brothers!
  Walking blindfold in the dark,
Know ye not how falsehood smothers,
. In your souls, each vital spark?
Will ye not arouse you, breaking
  From the bondage of the clay?
Long ago the morn was waking
  To a more transcendent day.

On the walls of heaven are walking
  Angels of immortal birth,
Bending down the azure, talking,
  Face to face, with souls on earth.
They have waited long, to bless us,
  Full of tenderness and care,
Scattering in our paths all precious
  Flowers of joy, that blossom where

6*

Love's celestial founts are springing,
　Nourished by ambrosial showers,
And all bright winged birds are singing
　In the incense-freighted bowers.
Ay, and they would greet us, telling
　Of the holier things they see,
In the glory-lighted dwelling
　Of Incarnate Deity!

Lo, a bridge of light is skying
　Death's transparent river-flow!
And the pebbles, under-lying,
　Glitter in the deeps below.
Never more shall it grow turbid
　From the storms of grief and care;
Unbelief no more disturb it,
　Nor the blackness of despair.

Even the bubbling of its foam is
　With a mystic charm endued,
And a bow of sweetest promise
　Hangs above it, seven-hued;
And the meaning of its flowing
　Waxes ever more divine,
And the sands, beneath it glowing,
　Are of pearl, and crystalline.

Sweetly flowing, tranquil river!
　Gliding, noiseless, on thy way,
Never more from thee, forever,
　Shall we shrink, in fear, away.

Oh, sweet river! as we're gliding
　So serenely down thy stream,
Seems it as in one abiding,
　All-entrancing, glory-dream!
Death, thou angel of pure brightness,
　Death, thou vision of delight,
Though our souls were ne'er so sightless,
　Thou wilt turn to day their night.

As a young babe, sweetly sleeping
　In the mother's fond embrace,
We consign unto thy keeping
　All the loved of time and place,
There is rapture in but thinking
　Of this river so sublime,
Where we'll stoop with angels, drinking
　In the blissful after-time.

Thus, oh, thus then, slowly drifting,
　Drifting, drifting, slowly on,
Where the glorious arch is lifting,
　Through which our beloved have gone,—

Underneath it floating slowly,
  Slowly floating, floating slow,
Through resplendent scenes of glory,
  Where melodious rivers flow,—

Now with swifter, swifter motion,
  Swaying with the swaying tide,—
Onward, to the shoreless ocean
  Of eternity, we glide!
Ocean, ruffled but by rimplings
  Of sweet airs from odorous Isles,
And the drowsy, dallying dimplings
  Of the wingéd zephyr's smiles.

Oh, so blissful are the gleamings,
  Gleamings of the bliss to be,
So delicious the dear dreamings,
  Dreamings of Eternity,
That the rapturous revealings
  Antedate their heaven in me,
And, in hallowing all my feelings,
  Flood them with sweet ecstasy.

THE BOQUET OF PINKS.

Pinks, beautiful pinks! ye have surely come,
In your fragrancy, fresh from my country home,
Far, far from the din of the city's strife,
Where redolent zephyrs are springing to life;
For there, in a sweetly sheltered spot,
Lies my childhood's cherished flower plot;
And pinks of my planting, now blooming there,
Breathe the very same perfumes on the air,
That are thrilling my senses with exquisite pain,
As I drink of your incense again and again;
And memory wakes in my innermost heart
Dim childish dreams, till I shrink and start
At the echo sweet of some long lost sound,
Or the deep'ning scar of some cruel wound.

LATENT JOY.

The hallowed hopes that over thee brood,
And the perfumed breath of thy womanhood,
As the blessed deeds of the true, and good,

Are shedding forever, around thy way,
An odor of sweetness, and love, that aye
Grows deeper, and sweeter, all the day!

I feel in a sacred, a charmed spot,
And into its depths I venture not,
Till my soul is redeemed from stain and blot.

A power of re-vision is over me cast;
I tread with thee through a darkened past,
Where gleams and glooms give a strange con-
    trast.

Is the sense of thy guardian's symbol clear?
Was thy childhood darkened with doubt and
    fear,
And hovering fogs, all damp and drear?

Was thy little bosom rudely tossed
By pangs relentless, and fond hopes crossed,
Till thy childish faith was almost lost?

Still canst thou remember sweet glimpses of
    blue,
When the sombre clouds let the sunlight
    through,
With shimmer, and glimmer, to cheer thy view?

And moments dawned when gladness came
Into thy heart, as a leaping flame,
And joy, bright joy! was no longer a name.

And at times a purpose, strong and high,
Shone on thy cheek and burned in thine eye,|
Aud that proud heart beat triumphantly!

I tremble, abashed, and am half afraid,
The dædalous paths of thy heart to thread,—
The secret heart of a fair, young maid!

And down, over many a sacred scene,
　Over many a closed, and hallowed spot,
Thy guardian angel drops a screen,
　And, with gentle tone, says, "Enter not."

But she silently points to a fearful weight
　That over thy heart's young hope was hung,
And tells how the cruel hand of Fate,
　From that heart, the bitterest drops hath
　　wrung.

She holds a wreath of thy past to me;
　Oh! say, is the garland's symbol true?
Mid the brightest buds, and blossoms free,
　Are cypress leaves, and the twigs of yew!

But sorrow itself hath a mission high;
　And Hope's defeats are not all in vain;
Some joy is latent in every sigh,
　Some pleasure responds to the keenest pain.

The past shall serve, as a winding stair,
  To action still more noble, and true;
And the galling chains of an old despair
  Hold the golden seal of a promise new !

RENUNCIATION.

GENTLY ! touch me gently, Brother !
  Ah, methinks thou now can'st see
All the grief I sought to smother,
  In my inmost soul, for thee.

Tenderly thy name is cherished,
  Faithfully thine honor kept,
But for evermore hath perished
  The strange passion, once which swept

O'er me, as a storm sweeps ocean,
  As a whirlwind, or a fire,
Kindling, to intense emotion,
  Every sensuous desire !

Every tendril of fine feeling,
  Seemed around thy strength to grow;
Every passionate revealing,
  Took a more impassioned glow,

Till my spirit-life seemed fading,
   Fading, withering, as a flower,
Which the hot hand of the Day King
   Clutches with too fierce a power.

Raise thou not a hushing finger;
   I must speak, and thou must hear!
Never an impassioned singer
   Chanted notes more deep and clear.

Had I loved thee truly, purely,
   I had never lost that truth;
Had thy love been wiser, surely
   Better were it now, for both.

Better! no; I would say, rather,
   It were better as it is,—
Better for the strength I gather,
   From a lesson learned like this.

For the troth kiss to thee plighted,
   Never could have been, to me,
Like the pure flame I have lighted
   At the fires of Calvary.

'Mid the jarring of my heart strings,
   Sweetest symphony awoke,
As when, with clear notes, a bard sings
   In a battle's storm and smoke.

And it calmed my every feeling,
  Soothed my passion's wildest cry,
Till each sense sank, reverent, kneeling
  At the Cross imploringly.

Oh, I pray thee, do not tarry,
  One memorial hour with me,
Since I never more can carry
  The old tenderness for thee.

As a stranger, stranger only,
  Do I clasp thy proffered hand,
And my feelings, gay or lonely,
  Thou canst never more command.

Go, I cannot need thy presence;
  Leave me, from this fleeting hour;
Or thy memory, as a pleasance,
  Will have lost its charméd power.

Let the dear old past be treasured,
  As a something sacred still;
I, its loftiest heights who measured,
  Its profoundest deeps can fill.

Of that past I learn to borrow
  Hope's serenest guiding star,
Not a rack of dark'ning sorrow
  Its effulgency can mar.

From that past a power is stealing,
　　Silently, and all divine,
And its holiest revealing
　　I have made forever mine.

Leave then, leave the few pale roses,
　　That within my spirit bloom,
For the hues their heart discloses,
　　And the sweets of their perfume.

Surely, pale and scentless seeming,
　　Must they be, to sense and eyes,
Gladdened by the gardens, gleaming
　　With the flowers of Paradise.

Go! these ears no more shall listen
　　To that winning voice of thine,
And these eyes no longer glisten
　　With pale feeling's treacherous sign.

For the future, now, must prove me
　　Strong in purpose, firm, and still;
Passion never more shall move me,
　　From the sceptred strength of will.

THE DIFFERENCE.

MEN speak of grief as if they were acquaint
  Therewith, or it were possible for them,
Though chastened by afflictions, e'er to paint,
  Or to conceive the woes, that as a flame,
Consume the heart of woman.   They do not
    Offer their heart's whole wealth upon Love's
    shrine ;
Altar and incense are too oft forgot,
  In striving with the world, delving the mine
For gold, or the poor purchase of a Name.
  She in her heart's devotion ever kneels,
Her offering burns in one undying flame ;
  Hiding her pain but his she knows and feels,
She lives, loves, hopes, and *dies* for him alone ;
  Woe, that such love and faith by man are
  overthrown !

CLARE AND LILLIE.

OH, I see your little Lillian !
  See your lily-bud so sweet,
Floating amid clouds vermilion,
  With all loveliness replete.

Oh, the soul-entrancing beauty
　Of the matchless Shining One!
We should bow in worship, could we
　Catch its full and perfect tone.

Angels shield my trancéd spirit!
　This is sure some glory-child,
Born of beings who inherit
　Natures pure and undefiled;
What a glory floats around her,
　What a gleam is o'er her spread;
With white lilies they have crowned her
　Meekly-bending, graceful head.

Locks, of sunny light are flowing
　O'er the whiteness of her brow,
While her dimpled hands are throwing
　Recognition towards us, now.
Father! mother! can your feeling
　Catch her presence bright and blest?
Does the beautiful revealing,
　Fill your souls with holy rest?

Lo, another spirit, bending
　Down the roseate serene;
Fuller maidenhood is blending
　In her graceful form, and mien;

Vails of gossamer are flowing
  Down her white limbs, to her feet,
And the zephyrs, round her blowing,
  Are all redolent of sweet.

Round her neck, and on her bosom,
  Hangs a fragrant garland bright,
Formed of every beauteous blossom
  Springing in Elysian light,
Crimson hyacinths, and roses,
  Mingle with the violet's bloom,
Even the myrtle here, reposes
  All forgetful of its gloom.

And this incense-breathing garland,
  Heaving with her bosom's swell,
Wakens visions of that far land,
  Where perfected spirits dwell.
In her left hand she is holding
  A fair tablet, ivory white,
With her right hand still unfolding
  Pictures radiant as light.

Now her snowy arm she stretches
  Up, toward the blue profound,
Then, with trembling hand, she sketches
  All the gorgeous scene around.

See her, see her, as she lingers
　Over each harmonious line,
See her slender, sunlight fingers,
　So translucently divine ;

Watch the changing of her features,
　Of her red lips' tuneful play,
'T would exalt even earthly natures
　To oblivion of their clay !
Now the fringéd lids are drooping
　Over eyes dark-luminous ;
She is stooping, slowly stooping,
　Now, methinks, she looks on us :
Ah ! she sees ! is recognizing
　For her face is heavenly fair,
Hear the blended voices rising,
　Of your Lillian, and Clare ?

Lo, the vision bright, advances ;
　Very near us are they now :
And the rapture of their glances,
　Sheds a light on either brow.
Joy a festival is holding
　On each brightening lip and cheek,
And their white arms interfolding,
　Seem to beckon as they speak.

Wait! a moment wait! until I
  Catch the words of that sweet pair;
List! "O, know you not your Lillie?"
  "Have you, then, forgotten Clare?"

SONG OF THE CHILDREN.

Ha, ha, ha! la, la, la!
  Ho, ho, ho, ho!
Lu, lu, lu! hu, hu, hu!
  Lu, lu, lu, lu!

Repletest, with sweetest
  And holiest power,
Caressings, and blessings,
  Upon you we shower.
Merrily, cheerily,
  Play we our parts;
Loving, improving,
  And gladdening, your hearts.

Ha, ha, ha! la, la, la!
  Keep to the chime;
Louder shout, as about
  Whirling in time.

Violette, Mignonette,
  Star-Beam and Mist;
Lily-Bud, Rosengood,
  Bright Amethyst!

Ho, ho, ho! so we go,
  See, as we fly,
Beautiful, musical,
  Waters run by.
Rivers deep, ever sweep,
  Tunefully sweet,
Dashing thus, luminous
  Globes at our feet.

Fairy-like, airy-like,
  Melodies flow,
Such, even, as in heaven
  The Glorified know.
The refrain breath again,
  Louder, more clear!
Let it blend, as we bend
  Over you, here.

Violette, Mignonette,
  Still swifter go!
Lily-bud, Rosengood,
  Thus let it flow.

Ha, ha, ha! la, la, la!
   Star-Beam and Mist,
Trip and sing, in our ring,
   Bright Amethyst.

Pebble-stones have their tones,
   Each one its own,
Gurgle-glad, murmur-sad,
   Laugh they, or moan;
Beauty-fraught is the thought
   Of the stream's daughters,
And they laugh, as they quaff
   Of the bright waters!

Mountain-tops, fountain-drops,
   And the rocks rude,
Have a speech, that would reach
   The deep solitude.
And the breeze, in the trees,
   Tells ever a tale,
As it drops from their tops,
   With a hum, to the vale.

There's a power, in each flower,
   To take from the heart
Its festering, pestering,
   Poisonous smart;

And to still any ill
    That to mortals may come,
And, for this, would we kiss
    Every beautiful bloom.

As we sing, see us bring,
    From our Elysian,
Wreaths so bright, that they might
    Glad a saint's vision;
Amaranth, Hyacinth,
    Blooms never sere;
Lily-bells, Asphodels,
    Bright through the year;

Rejoicing, in voicing
    Some hymn, that may tell,
Of a plain where no pain,
    For a moment, can dwell;
Where sorrow can harrow
    Remembrance no more,
Despairing and caring,
    Forever are o'er!

Where joy, no alloy
    Of its glory has shorn,
And the rose may repose,
    Unallied to its thorn;

And we children, in wildering
　　Dances, are whirled,—
The living, life-giving,
　　Sweet flowers of this world !

Mignonette ! Violette !
　　Star-Beam and Mist !
Rosengood ! Lily-Bud !
　　Bright Amethyst !
Ha, ha, ha ! la, la, la !
　　Trip it and sing,
Ho, ho, ho ! lo, lo, lo !
　　Whirl in our ring !

RUTH.

THE veined Wind-Flower in the sombre wood,
　　Thought breeding Pansies in the sunlight
　　　glowing,
　　Or red-cloaked Lilies in the meadows grow-
　　　ing,
Best image thee, in every changing mood;
For as the tricksy shadows all the while,
　　Keep dancing round us, in perpetual play,
　　So, o'er thy soul, its ever-changing sway
Fancy asserts.　Yet like a sea-girt Isle

Reason, deep-centred, sits, Majestic Queen!
  Though, all about, the wavelets gayly flash,
  On her white feet, with a perpetual dash,
She keeps her throne immutably serene,
  With an eternal sunshine on her brow,
  That sheds a rosy light on all the vales below

TO⸺.

Goᴅ of Heaven! what a throng
Of the Beautiful, the Strong,
And the glorious Sons of Song,
      Bursts upon my gaze!
What a light is o'er me shed,
As thy spirit-courts I tread,
And its mazy windings thread;—
      Still, the faintest haze
Rests upon the radiance bright,
So to temporize the light,
As to shield my dazzled sight
      From too brilliant rays.

Now I tread an Ocean-shore
Where Thought's billows, evermore,
An exalted music pour,
      Thrillingly profound;

8

With majestic strength replete,
White-maned Waves their marches beat,
Thundering on with surf-shod feet,—
  Glancing swiftly round,
Till some Reason-rock they spy,
When, with foam-crest mane tossed high,
With a loud exultant cry,
   'Gainst it, wild, they bound;
Stunned to madness by the blow,
Backward, as retreating foe,
The reluctant coursers go,—
  Making heaven resound
Their reverberating neigh,
Shaking from their flanks the spray,
Scattering, as they haste away,
  Clouds of gems around.

Now it changes to my view,
And the waters, then so blue,
Glow with every rainbow hue,
  Tremulously bright!
And they lie as calm and still,
With an all-pervading thrill,
As if God their deeps did fill
  With excess of light;

For in sudden, fitful gleams,
Lo, the radiancy streams,
As the glow of heavenly dreams
       Gilds the blackest night.
'Neath the ever-changing tide
Shoals of silvery fishes glide,
Monarchs of the deep beside,
       Kingliest in might.

Now beneath cerulean skies,
Trees of stateliest strength arise,
Fruit the rarest, ripest, lies
       Scattered everywhere :
O'er the flower-bespangled ground
Loveliest forms are gliding round,
To a most bewitching sound,
       Sweet beyond compare.
In the deepening, overhead,
Go the stars with regal tread,
By their royal Princess led,
       Where Night's monarchs are :
Star to star is wildly calling,
As with brilliancy appalling,
From that awful height they're falling,
       Like a rain of fire !

From these burning meshes, fraught
With intensest threads of thought,
What a fabric might be wrought,
     Than all earth-wefts higher.
Arbors of this boundless field
Choicest fruits and flowers yield,
'Neath its turf there lie concealed
     Gems, and rubies rare;
Brightest birds are o'er it winging,
Sweetest carols gayly singing,
To thy spirit ever bringing
     Sounds, which might inspire
Symphonies that could awake
Such deep echoes, they should make
The astonished earth to shake,
     As a wind-swept lyre.

With a hush-inspiring finger,
Evermore I'd linger, linger
Near one most impassioned singer,
     In this glorious band.
Oh, I pray thee, Spirit! pour
That entrancing music o'er,
Once again, and evermore!
     Will the music grand,

Waken visionings most high,
All divinest harmony,
All sublimest ecstasy.
          Under this control
Let me clasp some angel-hand,
Of the blessed, blessing band,
In the radiant spirit-land,
          Yielding up my soul.

FADED FLOWERS.

FADED flowers, I may not toss them
    Lightly from the vase away,
Each divinely whispering blossom
    Eloquent in its decay,
Still is swelling, with the welling
    Of its incense-burdened lay.

Prophecies fresh from the Angels,
    In your petals have I read,
Love's devout, inspired Evangels,
    With your odorous wings outspread,
In your whiteness and your brightness,
    Stand ye thus in Love's sweet stead.

8*

From the cluster, one pale trembler
　To my bosom would I take,
But I fear the shy dissembler,
　For the gracious Giver's sake;
With the ringing of its singing,
　Silenced hopes and joys might wake.

A LIFE SYMBOL.

Like some mighty river flowing
　Onward to the ocean blue,
In the sunshine brightly glowing,
　Gleams thy spirit on my view.
Backward, I its course can follow
　To the fountain whence it sprung,
In a quiet woodland hollow,
　Where the Fays and Dryads sung.

Oh, how tranquil and how quiet
　Was this sheltered little nook!
Seemed forever lingering by it,
　Joys, that brightest coloring took.
Wide its wealth of waters spreading
　To the sun's benignant smile,
Would it linger, softly shedding
　Light for lent light, back the while.

Darksome bank, and rock-ledge curbed it,
   Even in its earliest flow,
And rude rapids oft disturbed it,
   Through its depths and windings low.
Still forever faster, brighter,
   Sped it on its deep'ning way;
Even the murky dark grew lighter
   With clear promises of day.

Rose at length a towering mountain
   Full before the gentle stream;
Backward, to its primal fountain,
   Turned it, with a saddened gleam.
Then the darkness, and the sadness,
   Chilled its young activities,
Tempered all its gushing gladness,
   With pale sorrow's ebbing lees.

Still it might not linger, listless,
   Even in its native glen;
Flowing, but no more resistless,
   Stole it on, and on again;
But in spite of green hopes, blighted,
   And a young heart's cherished schemes,
Floating darkly, save when guided
   By the lurid lightning's gleams.

Yet to those who well can render
   The dim riddle of thy life,
Lurks the strength of manhood, under
   Stagnant calm, and stormy strife.
Starry thoughts out-twinkle keenly
   On the sky-arch of thy night,
And the moon, with lustre queenly
   Walks in feeling's softer light.

But the chilly night is ending;
   Swiftly comes the ruddy morn;
Swifter is thy life-stream, tending
   To its destined ocean-bourn.
On the hills, already, twitter
   Heralds of approaching day,
And the curls of morning glitter,
   Where the curtaining dark gives way.

Then, oh then, be strong and fearless!
   Mid thy fellows walk more bold;
For, before thy spirit peerless,
   Open glories manifold.
In the path of noblest duty
   Walk thou, with a manly tread
And the true life's holiest beauty
   Shall a glory on thee shed.

Lesser souls shall catch the assurance
   Then, that crowns thy life with bliss,
It will strengthen their endurance,
   Climbing crag, and precipice,
In endeavor stern, and trying,
   In the conflict with their wrongs,
Till from lips, all faint with sighing,
   Shall ascend triumphant songs!

Angel arms unseen infold thee,
   And the highest, supreme Heart,
As a child beloved shall hold thee
   Pledged to every noble part.
So I read the divination
   Of thy life stream's changing flow,
To the glorious consummation
   That the just alone may know.

THE ROSARIE.

Hark; it was their angel voices
   Which awoke that blissful strain;
My rapt spirit still rejoices
   At the jubilant refrain.

As from rosarie a maiden
　Golden beads drops one by one,
So their linked songs of Aidenn,
　Waken echoes, tone on tone.

As across the laughing meadows,
　Or where gurgling brooklets glide,
Sweep at noon, Sun-driven shadows,
　Steal these echoes, side by side.

HOPE AND FAITH.

DEAREST, though the angels told me
　Of the strength within thy heart,
Still, as closely I infold thee,
　Comes to mine a bitter smart.

I would soothe those throbbing temples,
　Cool the fever of thy brow;
Ah, the sunlight faintly trembles
　Through thy saddened spirit, now!

Like a stately city, standing
　By old Ocean's open door,
All its ceaseless strength commanding,
　All its treasures, evermore.

So thy spirit's calm reposing,
  Seemeth, to my spirit eyes,
As some crystal sea, inclosing
  All the sweets of Paradise;

Centred by a gleaming city,
  With its clustering domes and spires ;
And my spirit swells with pity
  At the sacrificial fires,

Burning on its temple altars,
  Gleaming on its golden shrine,
But the great sun never falters
  In its path of hyaline.

Be thou faithful, in thy bosom
  It shall kindle purer fires,
Making, in its depths, to blossom
  Higher, holier desires.

Bird-like melodies, the sweetest,
  In its dewy-dawn will start,
Pouring victory's completest
  Anthem, from thy inmost heart.

God himself gives inspiration
  To these choiring thoughts of **thine**;
Guard, then, every emanation
  From this origin divine.

Why thus saddened, beyond measure,
  In these clouds about thy way;
Oh, look up! and learn to treasure
  Stars that turn e'en night to day.

Wheresoe'er thou goest pouring
  Golden Hope, and beamy faith,
Till thy heart and soul are soaring,
  Victors over fate and death.

THE PROMISE.

I would my yearning heart could find a tone
Echoing responsive language to thine own,
Though in its far recesses I discern
The fires of love and gratitude that burn
On Friendship's altar, and behold, in thine,
The same sweet flame burn, lambent and divine,
Still, when expression's nobler flight I seek,
I find my tongue reluctant, slow, and weak;
My humble lyre no lofty song will bring,
But tones of sweetness vibrate on each string.
Restless ambition ever toils to bind
Her glittering chains upon the active mind,

But thou, exalted to some noble aim,
A brighter crown, a purer wreath may claim ;
Fronting so bravely all the ills of life,
And walking fearless through its wrongs and
    strife.
If thus, forever, thou canst hold in view,
The starry heights of a pure life, and true,
Thy future pathway shall be bright with bliss,
That far outweighs the martyrdoms of this ;
No clouds shall darken, with malignant frown,
But fadeless laurels thy white temples crown ;
Seraphs of beauty golden censers swing,
Love's holiest incense over thee to fling,
And, borne aloft on music's waves, shall soar,
Thy victor-soul, right on, for evermore !

AVE MARIA

Oʜ thou, my spirit friend,
Sweet mother ! as I bend
    Heart and knee,
Teach what my tongue shall say,
That I aright may pray
    Unto thee.

I would become more pure,
More willing to endure
    What may be;
Well knowing at my side
Whatever may betide—
    Guarding me,

Thy angel walks in light,
As walked thy Son by night
    On the sea!
And though my life-boat frail,
Rude tempest may assail,
    Wrathfully,

And waves tumultuous rise,
Threatening the pallid skies,
    In mad glee!
While fearful lightnings hiss
Down wave and precipice,
    Scornfully!

Yet will I feel no fear;
Oh, holy mother dear,
    Maid-mother free!
Thy sweet, assuring smile,
Rests over me, the while,
    Earnestly.

Sweet mother, mine, I pray,
Take not that light away;
    May it be
Within my inmost soul,
And all my thoughts control,
    Perfectly.

So holy is its power,
My soul can but adore
    Thine, and Thee!
The wisdom, love, and grace,
Which, from thy heavenly face,
    Beam on me!

WHAT THE ANGELS SAY.

SHALL I tell thee what the angels say,
   When in symbols they speak to me?
When they hover so lovingly over my way,
   And whisper strange stories of thee.

They bear me away to their heavenly bowers,
   In the freshness and fragrance of morn;
Thy spirit florescent, floats over the flowers
   That there, in bright beauty, are born.

In the indolent calm of a summer noon,
  In a reverie, fancy free,
Through Nepenthean odors, soft as June,
  They are wafting a vision of thee.

At twilight they take me on cloud-winged
      steeds,
  Where ripple the musical streams;
The amber-hued perfumes awoke in the meads
  Are the echoes of love-lighted dreams.

When the somnolent dews of the midnight
      weep,
  Weird protean fancies they twine,
A garland of Lotus-buds, sacred to sleep:
  To sleep and to dreams that are thine!

HUMAN LOVE.

FATHER in Heaven! permit me, as I may,
  To bring an offering, simple though it be,
Upon the shrine of human love to lay,
  Whereby my soul exalts itself to Thee.

Now bending low, I ask, imploringly,
   That I this silent power may never lose;
Then confident in faith, adoringly
   I gladden in the strength of its repose,—
The power that makes us more akin to Thee,
   The highest, sweetest power to spirits born,
To love, love only, even should there be
   For us, but wrong, injustice, hate and scorn,
Father, I pray Thee, may we ever prove
This Omnipresence of Omniscient Love.

FLOWER FAYS.

I WILL tell you of a vision,
   A vision of sweet power,
Which came from the Elysian,
   And was brought me by a flower.

For an hour, a whole hour,
   Above it I would bend;
Would you think a little flower
   Could have won your simple friend,

O'er its beauty frail, to ponder,
With an earnest child-like wonder.
And its leaflets fair to sunder,
          One by one?
       9*

Call it not a cruel part;
For, within its tender heart,
I had found a polished dart,
                    Thither thrown

By some merry-hearted boy,
In the recklessness of joy,
Never thinking 't would destroy
                    Its young bloom.

Oh, the rose did redly pout,
As I pulled the arrow out;
And it scattered all about
                    Its perfume,

Till the fragrance made me faint;
When with gesture, O, so quaint!
Breathed it out a low complaint,
                    In a song.

Sooth, I cannot give the air,
For it was, beyond compare,
Very wonderful and rare ;
                    And a throng

Came, of mischief-loving sprites,
Who in damp mid-summer nights,
Toss the ever-flashing lights,
                    In the vale,—

While the lonely whippowil,
From his bower beneath the hill,
All the listening air doth fill
   With his wail,—

They with mirth-provoking glances,
Wheeled round me in their dances
Their brows wreathed with bright pansies,
   Wet with dew.

Held each hand a cup of gold,
Wreathed in shapes of fairest mould;
And the quaintest tales they told,
   Which, if true,

I am sure I would not tell;
And if false, it were as well
That a silence o'er them fell,
   Tenderly.

So these I'll not recall,
Tho' the drapery of them all
Flutters, as a glittering pall,
   Over me.

But the moral of them is,
That thy life's distilled bliss,
Never might atone for this
   Wanton waste

Of the cherished sweets, that clung
Where my scented petals hung,
And to heaven their sweetness flung,
       Baby-chaste.

O gather gather one
Of the leaves so careless thrown ;
Let its sad, forgiving tone
       Plead its wrong.

For each leaflet, spreading fair,
Was the utterance of a prayer,
Which the flower gave the air,
       In a song.

'Gan the merry sprites to drink
From the tiny goblet's brink ;
At which one, with roguish wink,
       Drew more near;

And a saucy elf he was,
For he touched my shoulder, as
His thin treble, shrill as glass,
       Pierced my ear.

" To illume earth's darkened hours,
God," he said, "sends human flowers,
Human hearts from evil powers
       To beguile.

"And the aroma of sweet feeling
From them, mistily is stealing,
And the light of their revealing
        Is a smile."

But too oft they feign a part,
Feigning, till the fearful smart,
Of some unsuspected dart,
        Makes them feel

Something of the debt they owe
To the Heavens that bestow
Beauty's coruscating glow,
        Good and ill."

Then he laughed out merrily,
As he held his cup to me;
"This is nectar, drink!" said he,
        With a shout.

Then I heard their goblets clink,
Saw their little elf-eyes blink;
And they laughed, till one would think
        Such a rout

All their bloomy sphere must shake,
And its deepest caverns make
Merry mocking echoes take,
        For a time;

While the pool of lilies, thrilled
Through and through, its ripples stilled,
And the depths of air were filled
       With the chime.   ·

THE OAK.

TINY little ACORN! underneath the ground,
Working out a problem, solemnly profound!

Shoot of simplest beauty, frail as thou art fair,
Meekly giving utterance to the acorn's prayer;

Lightly springing Sapling, promising so much,
Ever swaying, gracefully, to the zephyr's touch;

Tree of fair proportions, slender, lithe, and
    strong,
Giving back the chorus of the wild wind's song;

Pride of all the forest, tree acknowledged king,
When the storms are loudest, when the tem-
   .pests bring,

From the dreary northland, all their fearful force,
And thy fellows tremble from their furious
    course;

Bald to rebel winter, garlanded in spring,
OAK! in all thy changes, nurtured to be king;

Regally majestic, thou dost wear thy crown,
Laughing loud, and scornfully, at the Storm-
god's frown.

THE EAGLE HEART.

As beneath the crystal waters,
  Diamonds glitter, very clear,
So thy mental sons, and daughters,
  Through their element appear,

In thy soul's serenest chambers,
  Reason's children make their home,
And Thought's sunlight, as it clambers
  To its blue, meridian dome,
Gilds, with loveliness transcendent,
  All thy high imaginings;
And the angel, thy attendant,
  Shakes ambrosia from her wings.

Thy soul's temple I have entered,
  And I linger at the shrine,
Where, in oriel-light, are centred
  The deep springs of the Divine.

Here are contrasts so united
  In all holiest marriages,
Strength to Gentleness is plighted,
  Pride to sweet Humilities.

O'er the sky came sudden changes,—
  Turns of Fate's Kaleidoscope;
To my spirit, as it ranges
  Over thine, there seems to ope
Scenes of glory, so entrancing,
  That I tremble as I view,
Lingering now, and now advancing,
  Through each thought-paved avenue.

As a dove might, young and tender,
  Find security, and rest,
For its pinions thin, and slender,
  In the fearless Eagle's nest,—

As beneath an oak wide-spreading,
  Nestles the sweet Eglantine,
As a rivulet, slow threading
  Its dark way, where rocks incline,
Suddenly in light emerges,
  Growing deeper and more clear,
Till it mingles with the surges
  Tumbling on the windy mere;

So all timid spirits, wrestling
   With the fearful storms of life,
To thy eagle soul fly, nestling
   From the tumult, and the strife;

So thy thought from doubt emerges,
   Growing deeper, and more clear,
Till it mingles with the surges
   Of the Everlasting mere!

THERE REMAINETH A REST TO THE PEOPLE OF GOD.

HEBREWS, IV. 9.

Sweet promise! the bruised and the sad ones
   of earth,
Who are sorrowing under affliction's hard rod,
This thought—oh, their bosoms may best know
   its worth;
  "There remaineth a rest to the people of
   God!"

10

Then cheer up, ye mourners, your tears wipe
    away,
  And lift your sad eyes from the mouldering sod,
Though the fruitage of joy, upon earth, may
    decay,
    "There remaineth a rest to the people of
      God!"

Tired pilgrim! oppressed and o'erladen with
    care,
  Who art toiling in sorrow o'er life's weary
    road,
Take courage, press on, never yield to despair;
    "There remaineth a rest to the people of God!"

And you, who in sorrow and suffering pine,
  On couches of sickness; though anguish cor-
    rode,
Let joy with your sorrow supremely combine,
    "There remaineth a rest to the people of
      God!"

Thou servant of Christ! who hast faithfully
    borne
  The yoke of thy Master, thy weary life-load,
Remember, though now a sad victim of scorn,
    "There remaineth a rest to the people of
      God!"

Oh exquisite rest! most holy, secure,
  To mingle for aye, in that happy abode,
With those we have loved, with the good, and
    the pure,
  This rest, holy rest, "for the people of God!"

MINISTRATIONS.

THERE are forms of beauty, bending,
  Ever bending o'er your way;
And they scatter blessings round you,
  As the night distils its dew;
And their presence lights your spirits,
  As the sunshine lights the day;
And no cloud of sorrow rises,
  But their soft eyes twinkle through!

There are angels bright, who linger,
  Ever linger by your side:
Ever watching, ever waiting,—
  Only watching for your good;
Their snow-white arms protecting
  You, if evil should betide,
Nourishing your hungry spirits,
  With their own ambrosial food.

In the noon-day there are voices,
Voices in the noon of night,
Which are whispering, of heaven,
Words of glory and of joy;
Oh, then listen, closely listen!
They will thrill you with delight,—
Stories of their blissfulness,
Of a bliss without alloy.

There are touches which are thrilling,
Thrilling with a power intense,
Through the inmost depths of feeling
Till ye know the hand that blesses,
As a holy consecration
Baptizeth every sense,
In the sweet, and sacred influence
Of their heavenly caresses.

There are most ecstatic visions,
Visions that like starbeams come;
While the tones of the departed
Waken holiest memories,—
Till there comes a childlike yearning
For your spirit's cherished home,
In the Father's blessed presence,
In the bowers of Paradise.

There are heavenly revelations,
 Revelations pure, and high,
That will flash athwart the spirit,
 Like the lightning's fierce control;
Giving glimpses of the glory
 Flashing on the inward eye,
Till a hallowed sense of blessing
 Lifts the transfigured soul!

REVERIE.

One summer evening, calm and still,
I sat upon a mossy hill,
And listened to the whippowil,
  Sad bird of night;

When came a voice, so soft and clear,
It fell upon my raptured ear,
Like music from another sphere,
  In dreaming heard.

It was a sound for earth too rare,
A sad-like, yet a joyous air;
I can, to nothing fit, compare
  That minor sound.
10*

Its vocal source I never knew;
It came upon me as the dew
Comes, and we ken not shape or hue,
    At shut of night.

But oh, it had a power to still
The ragings of the wayward will,
And deep, with holy thoughts to fill
    The trancéd mind.

I know that, from their holy home,
Exalted spirits oft will roam,
And to the haunts of mortals come,
    With power to bless;

But never, till that rapturous even,
Such grace was to my spirit given,
To feel, to taste, so much of heaven,
    So much of God.

LOVE'S IMMORTALITY.

Know, my loved ones, I am Ida:
    Ida who in Eden lives;
All the eve I've stood beside her
    Who my message softly gives.

I have lingered in your presence,
  Many a time, before to-night,
Shedding o'er your souls a pleasance,
  In a soft, inspiring light.

As the moonbeams, through the lattice,
  Will uncertain shadows cast;
As a sunlit vapor, that is
  Like a memory of the past;

As the drowsy vail of twilight,
  Shimmering in an eve of June;
As a waking love-dream's eye light;
  As the hidden wild bee's tune;

So, through earth-life's sensate curtain,
  Though your misty vision bent,
Gleams my presence, pale, uncertain,
  Distant-seeming, bright but faint.

Yet, my arms around you flinging,
  Long above you have I hung,
With a fond and tender clinging
  Round you, as in life they clung.

As in life? ah! I am giving
  Unto words an earth-like hue;
Never had I known of living
  Till I passed death's portals through;

Never known the god-like story
　Of the everlasting soul;
The immeasurable glory,
　That its destinies unroll.

O, my friends! I scarce know whether
　Most I love, or most adore,
This all-loving, holy Father,
　Who hath blessed me evermore.

And I quiver, as I name him,
　With an ever quick surprise;
To my lips come high, acclaiming
　Plaudits, thrilling to the skies.

And there come the clearest singing,
　Intertwining notes, that swell
All around me, and the ringing
　Pulses of a silver bell.

And a hymning low, and tender,
　Overflows and floods my soul;
Every thought it seems to render
　Strong, though sweet, in its control.

I have lingered unbelieving,
　In the broad, convincing light;
For it seemed like a deceiving
　Dream of beauty, fleet as bright,

That one spirit, thus, should enter
 To another's mortal home,
While that soul from its deep centre
 Over trackless fields might roam.

Yes, my friends, while I am speaking
 Through these trancéd lips to you,
Her unfettered soul is seeking
 Fields the senses never knew.

This unvails the sweetest mystery
 Life has lent me, even here,
This turns prophecy to history,
 Of earth's marriage with our sphere,—

Your old earth becomes less earthly,--
 Marriage holy and divine,
Of whose ritual high and worthy,
 Here behold the living sign;

Coming, as the soft caressings
 Of a mother's love below,
Coming, with the highest blessings
 Which the good in glory know.

Ask ye why, amid the pleasures
 Which are my attendants here,
I should seek to tread the measures
 That are trod upon that sphere?

Know the soul that loves, believing,
  Never loses aught it loves;
But, for evermore receiving,
  Ever takes, where'er it roves,
The distilled sweets of loving,
  The refined soul of sense;
And the heart grows richer, proving
  Love's repletest competence.

Therefore, purified, I carry
  All my earth-born tendernesses,
Thus I still delight to tarry
  'Mid love's flowery wildernesses,
And in heaven rejoice to marry
  Loving lips, in pure caresses.

THE JOY OF ACTION.

Thus beside thee as I linger
  Angel arms our forms entwine;
Each inspired, lovely singer,
  Chants a hymn of the Divine.
Most familiar is their greeting,
  Tenderly they press my hand,
All the while the slow time beating,
  With a shining silver wand.

Seems it as if I were dreaming,
  On a bed of poppies white,
Their low singing, and the gleaming
  Of the lithe wand, and the light.
Now a most enchanting essence
  Stupifies my every sense,
And I feel its witching presence
  Stealing through this sweet suspense.

But they go! they are ascending,
  Oh, sweet souls I half adore,
Bless ye, for the many blending
  Benisons ye on me pour.
They have left us to each other,
  Wilt thou suffer me to come?
I the flowers of thought will gather
  Blooming in thy spirit home.

What a strange, foreboding quiet,
  Seems to rest on all around,
Here's a lakelet, and anigh it
  Bright translucent shells abound,
Here are birds that are not singing,
  Fishes, but they do not play,
Nothing with swift gladness springing:
  Is it night, or is it day?

That thy soundless mental ocean,
 Like a sheet of silver spread,
Lies as listless, without motion,
 As if all its waves were dead.

Would'st thou rouse thy dormant powers
 To some action, true and high,
Startling, from these listless hours,
 All their blank vacuity,—
Sought'st thou, with a pure intention,
 Some good purpose to fulfil,—
Drawn to their extremest tension,
 All thy nerves with joy would thrill.
Work! there comes no angel bringing
 Deeper peacefulness than he,
Joy and health leap upward, singing
 In his regal company.

Thou art gentle, kind, and loving,
 And thy spirit is serene
As the gauzy, white clouds, moving
 'Twixt the azure and the green.
Need it were baptized in trial;
 Action should illume the shrine,
And the fires of self-denial
 Consecrate it, and refine.

What a heaven-descended dower
  Those deep sympathies of thine!
Thou should'st guard them, as a power,
  And a fellowship, divine,
That will lift thy soul to Heaven,
  Or bring that Heaven down to thee,
When to thy spirit shall be given
  Glimpses of Divinity.

LIFE'S MYSTERY.

LIFE in its various changes,
  Life in its phases rude,
Life in its highest ranges,
  Was never understood!

Life, when most staid and quiet,
  Life, when most crowned with **good,**
Life, howsoe'er we try it,
  Was never understood!

Life! over it, forever,
  Will doubt, and darkness **brood,**
And baffle man's endeavor,
  To make it understood.

11

Life! O, the Life of living,
  Its highest altitude,
Must ever be in giving,
  Were it rightly understood.

The soul's appointed mission,
  For which alone we live,
In high, or low condition,
  Is evermore to give.

In answer to our giving
  We evermore receive;
And, gratefully receiving,
  We fruitfully believe.

Belief is but ascension
  Unto the high and good;
And doubt, a sad detention
  By things ill understood.

Then grant us patience, Father!
  Whom many ills enthrall,—
For in ourselves we gather
  The sufferings of all.

But still as we are nearing
  Those clear, calm heights, and **true**,
Sweet voices are we hearing,
  And love-lights meet our view.

Oh, Life of our creation!
  It were a heaven to us,
Could we keep the high relation
  Distinct, harmonious,

Between the flesh and spirit,
  And of the soul to thee,
That the mansions we inherit
  As thy holy courts may be.

LITTLE MOSS ROSE.

A LOVELY rose-bud in the sunshine glowing,
  Simple and modest, and as sweetly wild,
  As though young Zephyr nursed it as her child,
Art thou wee Pet; so innocently growing
Upon the parent stem, while sun and dew
  Still foster thee, with care the tenderest,
  And spirits hover over the green nest
Which shelters thee. Ah, budling fair and new,
Be thou not tempted from this safe retreat,
  By the gay sunshine of the world alluring,
  Where prouder beauties glance with more
      assuring
Effluence and color, but how far less sweet
  Than thou bright blossom, O then linger here
  God and his angels are so very near.

THY MOTHER.

A BRIGHT Figure, beaming
In the rose-light of dreaming,
Seems folding us close in embraces of love;
   Ah, see! 'tis none other
   Than thy beautiful mother,
Bending lovingly down from the silence above.

   Oh, say, canst thou hear her?
   Come nearer! come nearer!
Her tones are so mellow, low, soothing, and
     sweet;
   Each sense I surrender
   To an influence tender,
And sink in a rapture of bliss at her feet.

   The tenderest blessings,
   The sweetest caressings,
That ever a mother on daughter did shower,
   All pure consecrations,
   All high aspirations,
She lavishes on thee, unchanged with the hour,

Her love-light will strengthen
When dun shadows lengthen,
And life's stilly evening succeeds to its noon,
When day, with its hid light,
Sinks starless to midnight,
Her love will be o'er thee for planet and moon.

Her exquisite spirit
Must surely inherit
A home of rich beauty and loveliness rare,
For, dimly beholding
Her glorious unfolding,
I see a clear flush in the scintillant air.

And a sense of contrition,
And lowlier submission
Grows strong in my soul with my strengthening
faith.
Oh is it but seeming,
Illusion and dreaming?
Or have I gone up through the portals of death?

With rapturous singing
The angels are winging
In circles resplendent, or poised in the air;
Oh, Infinite Father!
From thee I would gather
New strength, by new virtue, their glory to bear.

11*

PAULINE.

WHITE browed Anemones, daughters of the sun,
 And blue-eyed violets, with the mignonette,
 And pale pink roses with the valley's pet,
The myrtle, iris, lily, every one
Becomes a sweet Interpreter of thee;
 And as I list the voices of thy soul,
 So soft and gentle, yet in their control
Strong and subduing, clearly do I see
The latent strength that slumbers in thy spirit,
 Where lofty faith and aspirations high,
 And holy loves keep closest company,
Building the heaven predestined souls inherit.
 Oh, the sweet influence of thy soul on mine
 Is as an effluence of the most Divine!

YET ONCE AGAIN.

YET once again, most joyfully, I come
Within the circle of thy soul's high home.
Again I bend, my spirit brow to lave
In healing waters from the crystal wave
Of thy deep ocean of exalted thought,
With power-inspiring power as richly fraught.

As the famed pool Bethesda could have been,
Save when the influence of the Nazarene
Rested upon it.   Still dwells with thee such
Blessed divinity of angel touch,
As, in its worth, might almost rival, even
That which adorned the glorious Son of Hea-
 ven,—
For as Heaven's Son we ever recognise
The lowly Jesus,—though our spirit eyes
See other sons of Heaven, less good, less pure,
Less perfect, yet as willing to endure
The martyrdom of suffering and of shame,
That comes to all who dare assume a name
Which the false years presumptuously con-
 demn,—
The mocking years, bow not, my soul, to them
Bigots and tyrants, fell and treacherous,
Forever cry " Ye shall not rule o'er us!"
To the pure spirits, who, with holiest love,
Their wicked, sensual, selfish deeds reprove. ·
Redeemers, Saviors, we ne'er recognise,
Until the mission of their high emprise
Hath been perfected, then, the blind may see,
Clustering about them, their Divinity.

My spirit-brother! Shall I call thee such?
Emboldened by the sweet, inspiring touch

Of thy soul's finger, seeming to impart
Sublimest teachings to my kindling heart,
Thrilling my lips as with celestial fire,
Waking my soul to aspirations, higher
And holier, than any I have caught
From lips, unless by inspiration fraught.
Thy earthly raiment now is rent away,
I see thee all divested of thy clay,
And read thy spirit, as I read a book;
Through all its inmost mysteries I look.
As sparkling bubbles on a limpid stream,
In the soft moonlight beautifully gleam,
Or as the wavelets on the ocean's blue,
With silvery gleamings, fascinate the view,
As sportive sylphs, by their bewitching dance
O'er the bright waters, every eye entrance,
Along its course thy life-stream ever glides,
Watering the simplest herbage by its sides,
Foam-wreaths of Fancy, o'er its surface fly,
Feeling's fair lilies in the sunbeams lie.
Meandering now through blooming meadows
    fair,
Where spring the flowers of science, rich and
    rare,
Through forest thick, where Wisdom's stately
    trees,
Lift their high branches to the swelling breeze;

Anon through valleys shady, quiet, low,
Mid thirsty plants and hungry roots to flow;
Then on a fruitful, far-extending plain,
It spreads its bosom to the sun and rain,
That it may give the healing draught again
To thirsty mortals, who, devoid of sight,
Walk blindfold, ever groping for the light.

What a strange study is thy soul to me;
Simple and clear, yet full of mystery,
A subtle link unites it to the earth,
A tie half human, half divine in birth;
Yet is the bond so subtle and so slight,
They stand apart, dissevered in my sight.
If, on thy actual hand, or heart, or brow,
I place my actual hand, as I do now,
An answering throb, in unison most clear,
Gives an assurance thou art of this sphere;
But if my spirit hand I clasp with thine,
The inspiration makes us both divine,
And in a circle, sweeping far above
Earth's narrow limits, hand in hand we rove,
Through most transcendent, glorious abodes,
Into the presence of the God of gods!
And feel our spirits sweetly harmonize,
In all perfections growing great, and wise.

HERO-SOUL.

Oh hero-soul, Life's temple dost thou build,
   Arches and columns, towers and glowing
      spires;
With incense of good deeds its halls are filled,
   And love to God kindles its altar-fires.
Ah me! I know full well, to souls like thine,
   With every dawn there evermore doth come
Some sacrifice to lay on Duty's shrine,
   Some sterner conflict, deeper martyrdom;
And Pity's tears are falling, as I think
   Of all the sorrows gathering on thy way;
From what a cup of anguish must thou drink,
   What dizzy heights, what dismal depths survey.
From out so black and storm-conflicting night,
There must be born a day of radiance bright.

THE HEALING GIFT.

Angels of mercy, from Love's inmost shrine,
Did at thy birth a fadeless laurel twine,
Around thy spirit's pure transparent brow,
Lending all sweet perennial flowers that blow,

For thy green chaplet, full of odors sweet,
And with all healing potencies replete.

Yes! it is true, thou did'st the power receive
Largely, all pain and anguish to relieve,
Controlling all the demons of disease,
While prescient sufferers eagerly would seize
Thy healing hand, upon their hearts to press,
Taking new vigor from its soft caress.

Behold, sweet sister! see anear thee stand
A shining angel with a silvery wand;
Slowly he waves it over earth and sea,
Then gently lays the crystal point on thee,
With touch resistless in its strong control,
Nerving the feeblest purpose of thy soul.

Still more impressive grows the heavenly scene
By the bright presence of the Nazarene,
In whom supreme the healing gift was found;
His glorious brow with martyrdom is crowned,
And, kindly bending from the calm above,
He folds thee closely in his arms of love!

Prize of thy generous heart and lofty deed,
Thine is the sacred gift, the exalted meed,
Some soothing cordial on each wound to pour,
Some healing balm, for every suffering hour

That earth's afflicted sons are doomed to know,
In their wide wanderings through this vale of
    woe.

Sad hearts are gladdened by thy cheering tones,
As the lone widow, by Maria's son's;
Fulfil thy mission, wearying though it be,
Jesus himself shall walk the path with thee;
Angels of love on all thy steps attend,
And pitying souls their sweetest succor lend.

Guard, as the fortress of thy sacred wealth,
The priceless remnant of that shattered health;
Keep all thy steps with vigilance and care,
In even hands the healing cup to bear,
That so pure clay to purer soul allied,
By its own glory is most glorified.

PROPHET BARD.

POET and Brother, loved and honored, more
    Than thy heart counts amid its treasured gains,
Stint not, oh Prophet Bard, thy soul to pour
    Even on barren fields, like Autumn rains:
Thou might'st have built a throne where, long
    before,
    Fame would have sat, amid the echoing strains

Of thy own harp; had'st thou, more world-wise
   sung
Some mouthing Patriot's eulogistic rhyme,
Some high-born dame's or maiden's praises rung,
   As a lithe trifler trolled an idle chime,
Or, with less zeal of earnest passion, felt
Thy gift's high sanctity, at random thrown
Truths taught by Nature, where thy spirit knelt,
   But even yet, proud Fame shall claim thee as
   her own!

FORESHADOWINGS.

Though I know thou art not seeking
   For the things I now rehearse,
Yet am I impelled to speaking,
   And the utterance comes in verse.

Thou art formed for highest uses,
   Though, upon thy mental skies,
Hang the clouds of dark abuses,
   Clouding o'er the bright sunrise
Of that Faith, which should enlighten
   All the future, to thy tread,
While the stars of Hope that brighten,
   Melt in glory over head!

For I feel this strong assurance,
   That within thy noble heart
Burn the fires of true endurance,
   That to others might impart
Strength to conquer the conspiring
   Enemies of Truth and Right;
Courage, faith, and love refiring
   At thy own heart's altar-light.

Tenderly the dawn reposes
   On thy spirit beauty-crowned,
And the breath of full-blown roses
   Sheds their fragrances around.
Reason stands like oaks majestic,
   Stalwart, leafy sentinels
Casting shadows, most fantastic,
   Over all the flowery dells.

Now their leaves, in blithe carousing,
   Dance, and drink the dew-drops rare
And, anon, hang, faintly drowsing,
   In the incense-freighted air.

Noble cities, grand and stately,
   With full many a teeming mart,
Mountains towering up sedately—
   Nature's wonder-works of art;

Every thing in earth, air, ocean,
  I have seen reflected here,
In minute, but just proportion,
  Forming an harmonious sphere,
Where thy sun, with perfect glory,
  O'er a cloudless noon shall shine,
And fleet angels bear the story
  Of the morning's birth divine.

Oh, I hear their gladsome singing,
  See them with bright garlands crowned,'
While the vaulted heavens are ringing
  With the rapture-pealing sound.
See the countless millions gather!
  Oh, I shudder, shiver, sink;
Shelter! save me, Heavenly Father!
  Still, forbid me not to drink
From these waters of the Elysian,
  On whose hills of broader scope,
To my soul's anointed vision,
  Scenes of deeper glory ope;
Giving those intense revealings,
  Which the sight can scarce endure;
Consecrating all my feelings,
  With baptisms high and pure.

Seems as from me life were fleeing,
　God's effulgence so doth fill
Every inlet of my being,
　With an all-pervading thrill.

Dearest Father! thou hast told me
　We were of Thyself a part;
Oh, then, as an infant, fold me
　Near to thy sustaining heart;
Still permitting that I cherish
　This sweet vision; let it stay
As a light that cannot perish,
　Dawn of thy eternal Day.

RIVAL CLAIMS.

Never knew I harp so changing
　As this spirit lyre of thine,
Now, where angel hands are ranging,
　Now where fingers less divine.

Here a tone of triumph taking,
　Self-reliant, calm, and strong;
There with terror weakly shaking,
　Pouring a complaining song.

Strangest discord quivers through it;
　Thrills a harmony sublime;
Loving sympathies subdue it
　To a gentle, tender chime.

Now imbued with deepest sadness,
　Then with passionate desire,
Soon, intoxicating gladness,
　Vibrates on the trembling wire.

Oh, 'tis piteous! thus to squander
　An inheritance so high,
Thus to vacillate, and wander,
　'Twixt the lights of fen and sky.

Learn to prize the holy treasure
　In thy deep heart slumbering,
Tune thy lyre to some fixed measure,
　Some star-centred rhythm sing.

Maiden, blushing the confession
　Of the virtues in thy breast,
With thy womanly expression
　In the sweetest accents dressed;

In thy gentle nature blending
　Every captivating grace,
And the rival charms, contending
　In thy ever-changing face,

12*

Thou art regal as a queen is,
   Hast withal as rich a dower;
Would'st thou teach thy heart sereneness,
   Then were thine a queenly power.

Then arouse thee, gentle sister!
   Life is far too brief an hour
For our souls to dwarf its vista,
   By the wasting of a flower.

Rival crowns I see before thee—
   One of pure and true desire,
One, if once it glitters o'er thee,
   It shall cling like chemic fire.

Take the star-crown of the Father;
   Spurn the tempter's diadem;
And thy coming days shall gather
   Power and Peace, perfecting them.

MY WIFE.

Oh blame me not, May, that so long I delayed
My coming to greet thee; my footsteps were
   stayed

By a lingering fear that thou would'st not be-
    lieve
The words I might speak, or it haply might
    grieve
Thy sensitive nature, my Beautiful One!
Yet dearest, believe me, thou art not alone.
I linger above thee, by day and by night,
I share in thy sorrows, and in thy delight.

There are times when my presence has over
    thee thrown
An influence of sweetness thou canst not dis-
    own.
There are times when I hold thee within my
    embrace,
And gaze, as at first, on thy love-lighted face:
There are times when old feelings within thee
    are stirred
Till thou thrillest with rapture, my beautiful
    Bird!

Be patient, be hopeful, let what will betide;
There are spirits of beauty who walk by thy
    side.
I will come to thee, Mary, will over thee bend
As a guardian angel, thy steps to attend;

Bright joy to thy life I will evermore bring,
And aye to my strength shall thy gentleness
　　cling.

Then deem it no weakness to cherish a love
For thy young heart's betrothed, though his
　　home be above,
To live in the bliss of his loving caresses,
For thee with delight he embraces and blesses.
May love, joy, and peace, be the crown of thy
　　life,
And death bring my Mary, my darling, my wife!

FREED !

FATHER, I thank thee! Thou hast called my
　　child
　　Back to thyself, and to its home in heaven !
No more above his bed, in anguish wild,
　　　Through the dark night-hours will my prayers
　　　　be given;
No more at day-break will the dreaded horn,
　　　From the sick sufferer, summon me away;
No more, from his embraces rudely torn,
　　　I go, despairing, to my gloomy day !

'T was a rich gift, O Father, that proud boy;
　　Gladdening my bosom with his eye of light;
And though in him was centred all life's joy,
　　Over its beauty hung a nameless blight!
But now, my bliss is mixed with no alloy;
　　Now is my darling born an Angel free, and
　　　　white!

AN ADMONITION.

With thy soul is earliest morning,
　　And the dew lies on the ground,
While a glory, all-adorning,
　　From the sun is poured around.

In thy bosom playful fancies
　　A beguiling sweetness shed,
As the odors of young pansies
　　'Neath the sportive Fairies' tread.

Half-blown lilies are revealing
　　Snowy busts in bodice green,
Buds of tenderest thought and feeling
　　Half-expanded, bloom between.

Like bright bubbles, gayly flashing
   On some streamlet as it flows,
Or as ocean wavelets plashing
   In the noon of night's repose;

As the laughing sylphs, advancing
   In their revels, full of glee,
With the flashing billows dancing
   To the morning's melody;

As fresh grasses in the meadows,
   As the shadows on the hills,
As the twittering of young sparrows,
   As the incense noon distils;

As the breath of blooming clover,
   Glances of red berries bright,—
So around, beneath, and over;
   All thy soul is a delight!

But I give thee earnest warning
   That its weapons are too fine,
Less for conflict than adorning,
   Sterner metal should be thine,

Fit to strengthen and ennoble
   All the future of thy life,
Arming for the day of trouble,
   Arming for the day of strife.

INVOCATION.

BEAUTIFUL spirits, gloriously fair !
Fondly ye hover round the loved one there,
In the stern strife from love and home afar
Where the grim legions of the Alien are;
Yet he beholds not, though ye come so near:
Can ye not, spirits, make his vision clear,
Lift from his weary hand his drooping head,
And from that breast, to saddened fancies wed,
Drive the dark spirit of distrust and dread
And dry the tears his weary eyes must shed.
Ye can the Wanderer of his pangs beguile,
And light his dim'd eye with a radiant smile,
Make his still heart with hopeful joyance spring
And lend old gladness an exultant wing,
Draw the dark future's clinging vail away,
And fill his soul with promises of day,
That he its kindling raptures may behold,
Pleasures unthought, and ecstasies untold.

Now as ye wheel in mazy circles round,
He starts! he listens! yes, he hears the sound
Of the glad notes your choirs are chanting now,
See, what a glory sits upon his brow !

With what delight are his quick pulses thrilled,
With what enchantment is his bosom filled!
Now to the Father—forced no more to roam—
In dreams of Heaven his spirit flutters home,
Leans on the Saviour in a blissful thought;
With joy we leave him to the spell ye've
 wrought.

Ah, see! he kneels, he bows in fervent prayer;
To him, sweet sisters, let us draw more near,
Pour a full blessing on his youthful head,
And heavenly love like balmy incense shed.
As his soul hungers for the joys of heaven,
Give him to feel his sins are all forgiven;
And as his spirit calmly sleeps in bliss,
Just touch its red lips with a parting kiss;
Once more a heartfelt blessing we renew,
And turn to leave him with a blithe adieu.
Beautiful Spirits, hasten not away!
Leave, leave with me a blessing too, I pray;
And ere the dying of that farewell strain,
Promise me, Spirits, to return again,
Or that I meet you in the realms of **air**,
Beautiful Spirits, gloriously fair!

PHANTASY.

"Tiny Acorn"
Was the first born
Of the friendship felt for thee;
Then the proud oak
Still more loud spoke
To thy inmost soul of me.

Gentle Lady,
I conveyed thee
Many thoughts thou lovest well,
And have brought thee
Every thought free,
Thus to hold thee in my spell.

Life's hard lesson
Finds expression
In the ripple of these rhymes,
As a river,
Flowing ever,
Murmurs out its dreamy chimes.

In the dead light
Of the midnight,
I have sought thee as thou slept;

When the gleamings
Of bright dreamings
Have across thy bosom swept.

Oh surrender
Every tender,
Lofty feeling of thy soul,
Each upspringing
Fancy winging
Onward to this glorious goal.

Brighter beauties,
Higher duties,
Will the future bring to thee.
Oh, be careful,
Watchful, prayerful,
Thus to keep thy spirit free.

I am twining
With this rhyming
For thy brow a holy wreath,
Pure and fadeless,
From the shadeless
Flowers beyond the shores of death.

Radiating
Consecrating
Odors pure, and high, and good.

Near the Father
Thou shalt gather
Heavenly manna for thy food.

I STOOD BESIDE THEE.

I STOOD beside thee all that night of grief
Longing, but powerless, to bestow relief;
Still all untroubled, for I saw how clear
The sun of Trust would rise again, to cheer.
The wrong and doubtful from the true and right
Will fade, as darkness fadeth from the light.
On a spring's bosom did'st thou never trace
Perfect reflections of thy form and face;
Did'st never see some leaflet flutter down
On its fair surface? thus, sometimes, is thrown
A ruffling shadow o'er the depths of mind,
Blurring an image faithfully enshrined.
A breath will dim the purest mirror's face,
So may a thought, from other minds, efface
From thy dear soul the messages we send,
Or if not all, some mist may with them blend,
Leaving their beauty but in fitful gleams;
A troubled slumber giveth troubled dreams.

THE DEAD BABY.

A SPIRIT approached that I knew not before
Who sang me this lay of the baby she bore.

"This child on my bosom, but yesterday clung
To the breast of its mother, who joyfully sung
Such rich baby-lays, that the seraphs above
Bent o'er the blest twain, in transports of love.
The child raised its eyes to the jubilant band,
And with gleeful surprise it threw up its white
    hand
With a beckoning gesture, as if it would fain
Woo the beautiful beings from heaven again.

"Then they hovered still nearer the mother and
    son,
So near that the child caught their low under‑
    tone.
A moment, all motionless over the pair,
They hung in a silence, profound as the prayer
A dying saint offers, unuttered, to God,
Ere his spirit departs for its blissful abode.

"Then, fleet as the lightning, or cherubim fair
With wings ever brightening the tremulous air

Came down to the baby, so softly anear,
And whispered a mystical word in his ear;
Then the red on his cheek grew white as the
snow,
His pouting red lips lost their rich, ruddy
glow;
O'er the love-beaming eyes the veinéd lids
close,
His dimpled hands fold like the leaves of the
rose.
Unbroken the vigil that mother still keeps,
As she thinks, how profoundly her little one
sleeps!

" Oh, blissful young mother; alas! for the joy,
The pride, hope, and love, centred all in thy boy!
The soft, tiny hand, thy warm fingers enfold,
To ivory stiffening, grows ivory cold.
She bent her quick ear, his low breathing to hear.
Oh God! how she shook with a shivering fear!
No sweet coming breath, from his lips, met her
own,
And the little plump cheek was as cold as the
stone;
The blood to her heart shuddered back with a
bound,
And she sank, a new Niobe, smote to the ground.

"Oh, blissful reprieve from the swift-coming
    woes!
Too soon, yet too soon, from that trance she
    arose,
Locked around her dead babe, firm as steel is
    her grasp.
In vain is the struggle her hands to unclasp,
She hears not, she sees not, she deigns no replies.
But frantic and wild are her heart-rending cries.

"'I will not believe it! this cannot be death!
He is sleeping, sweet baby! I hear his low breath;
See, how closely he presses his cheek to my
    breast;
Oh, do not, I pray you, disturb his calm rest!
Hard-hearted! ye never shall pile the cold clod,
'Twixt my baby and me, oh! forbid it my God!'

"Poor grief-stricken mother, 'tis well, for the day,
That thy senses, bewildered, should wander
    away.
But when they return, may they gladden, to
    hear
The voice of thy darling resound from the
    sphere,
Where, crowned with Immortelles, and vestured
    in white,
He walks with light angels, an angel of light!"

GUARDIAN ANGEL.

A MOTHER is bending, with love-light descending,
  From her sunny, sweet face, o'er a daughter
    as fair;
And oft, in extreme night, her touch gives the
    dream light
  That cheers her in slumber, or lightens her care.

With holiest feeling, that mother is kneeling
  In prayer without ceasing, effectual, deep;
Some gentle revealing, at times must be stealing
  O'er the heart of her daughter, if only in
    sleep.

Oh, yes! I behold now, a light on her cold brow,
  That lends a conviction my vision is sure,
Oh then, ever careful, be watchful, and prayerful,
  To heed well a guidance so loving and pure.

Her spirit hath crowned thee with strength, that
    around thee
  Hath kindled a light, in thy darkness so drear,
Oh, heed then, her warning; be the noon to thy
    morning
  Effulgent in beauty, in purity clear.

Let no sin of omission, no deeds for contrition,
  Between her pure spirit and thy spirit come;
But ever as now, bear untarnished thy brow,
  And forgetful of heaven, she will rest in thy
    home!

A SPIRIT-MOTHER'S PRAYER.

'TIS thy mother! and she presses
  Her white hand upon thy head;
Pure the light of her caresses,
  As the perfume roses shed.
Claspéd are those hands in prayer,
  As in earnest, pleading tone
She beseeches,
        "Have a care
God Almighty for my son,
Let thy blessing, holy Father,
  Ever, ever on him rest;
Strength and courage may he gather
  From each trial; to thy breast
Father, clasp him, and thy love
  As a mantle round him folding,
Shield him from the hungry drove—
  Foes that, even now, are holding

Revels in their secret chambers,
   In the castle-holds of wrong:
May Truth's sunlight, as it clambers
   To the roof-tree, be more strong
Than the falsehoods that would wrestle
   From the wronged the right away;
May the dove of promise nestle
   In his heart of hearts, alway!

" Well I know he will not palter,
   Pledged he stands for truth and right;
Well I know he will not falter
   In the thickest of the fight.
But, oh Father, holy Father!
   Most unequal is the strife,
See'st thou not how thickly gather
   Tempest clouds along his life?
Will they not, ere long, come breaking
   Over his belovéd head ?
Day by day the storm is waking
   To fresh anger, and its tread
Booms as heavy as the thunder,
   And its glance of vengeful ire,
As when lightning darts from under
   Thickest blackness, flashing fire!

" Father keep him, oh, I pray thee
   Let his faith and love endure;

Let his strength still as his day be,
   God thy promises are sure:
Thou hast said that thou would'st take him
   Under thy especial care,
And I know thou'lt not forsake him,
   Hear, oh hear a mother's prayer.

" 'Tis in vain I seek to smother
   This too apprehensive love;
' Oh! forgive, forgive a mother
   If, for such a son, she prove
Anxious in her earnest praying,
   Reckless of all other care;
Fearful lest this base betraying
   Scourge him on to flat despair:
Scourge him as the angry ocean
   Scourges the resounding shore;
Oh, amid each wild commotion
   God protect him evermore!"

EVA.

THE pulses of thy being, fold the silences
Most reverently about them. Thy heart
Is hushed by Solitude's profoundest stillnesses,

And through the inmost depths of thy awed
    spirit,
Sacred repose steals softly as in dreams.
                Or worshipping,
Obediently bends, clasping its hands
In an unspoken prayer, nor ever lays
Its robes of glory by, because, for ever,
Its recognition of the Infinite
Falters not, in the silences of thought.
Beyond description, is it sweet and strange,
This spiritual influx, flooding the soul
With radiant glory-beams, a sea sublime
Of wisdom-lighted billows; to revel
Mid the flashing wavelets of conceptions
Lofty and pure, as heavenly dreams can give.
A twilight scene is now outspread before me;
I seem to thread thy future. Everywhere
Above thy head, are gleaming stars which yet
Will shed a radiance holy, that shall shower
On thee, and on the world, intensity
Of Truth's high power, and Love's all-conquer-
    ing might.
Were not thy spirit as an open book,
I could not thus peruse it.
                'Twere in vain
To seek concealment of a single syllable,
So perfect their succession each on each,

In their connection so symmetrical,
And like a well-tuned instrument, according,
If the key note be touched but skilfully.
Then throw at once this modest screen aside,
   And suffer all to read thee just as clear,
That with bright beauty, all be satisfied;
   And loving hearts, who linger thus anear
Thy captivating presence, be aware
Of the pure under current swelling there.
In whose intenser depths, serenely float
Voices the careless ever fail to note,
Lured by the mist-wreaths, and the lustrous foam
Of the soul's surface, from the thoughts which
      come
Through angel voices, unto mortals given,
When inspiration opes the gates of heaven,
And Christ, the Beautiful, bends meekly down,
Their asking spirits with his love to crown.

————————

THE NEW REVELATION.

FROM highest Heaven a spirit voice, to-night,
   Speaks to my soul, in accents fine and clear,
   List for a moment, gentle friends, and hear
The tones come, fluttering as the boreal light;

And now I catch the burden of the theme.
" Rejoice, that earth beholds a better day,
And Heaven is opened through a surer way
   Than flitting shadows, and imperfect dream !
Ye hear the whispers of the Angel-band,
   With God himself ye hold communion high,
And feel the consecration of his hand,
   The inspiration of his cloudless eye !
Oh, be ye faithful, ye who are believing,
Perfect your spirits for more full receiving."

NELL.

As a full blown orange flower,
   As a pure white lily-bell,
As a dark eye's matchless power,
   Art thou, O most beauteous NELL !

As the whisperings of the twilight,
   As the wavelet's gentle swell,
As the mysteries of the midnight,
   Art thou, O mysterious Nell !

As a bright-lipped Fairy-maiden,
   Dancing o'er a flowery dell,
With all witching fancies laden,
   Art thou, O bewitching Nell !

14

As the fresh breath of the morning,
　　As the fullnesses, that dwell
In the noontide's rich adorning,
　　Art thou, O most glorious Nell!

As the sweet hymn of a blossom,
　　As a soft-toned silver bell,
As the incense-freighted bosom
　　Of the rose, art thou, dear Nell!

As the winking of bright star-beams,
　　The strange histories they tell,
The revealings of our rare dreams,
　　Ever art thou, dreamy Nell!

Ripplings of the moon-lit ocean,
　　Sunbeams in a crystal well,
Every trancéd, trancing motion,
　　Images my graceful Nell!

Oh, the witchery of thy glances,
　　Of thy red lips' matchless spell,
Of the light and shade, that dances
　　O'er thy face, thou saucy Nell!

Won, by woman, down from Heaven,
　　Poets sing, that angels fell,—
Blameless, had their charmers, even
　　Half thy glory, queenly Nell!

A VISION.

JUST as my spirit left its clay, this eve,
 And darkness settled down;
And my whole being seemed dissolved in air,—
Thrilled on my spirit ear a music-strain
Soothing and sweet, and on its mellow waves
There came faint gleamings of the palest light,
 Pervading all my thought-sky.
Star after star, came leaping with glad smiles,
Into this realm of song, and all the heavens
With glory-beaming brightness were aglow!
In this effulgence, kindred to the light,
 Or as it were the light,
 The music rose and fell;
Now soaring to profound sublimities,
Anon to all sweet cadences descending.
Instinct with life, it seemed, and bore me up,
 On its irradiant wings,
Into the realms of perfectness and peace;
How shall I speak that perfectness and peace!
 Wrapped all around, and as it were,
Steeped, in their most ethereal influences,
My spirit, drooping with the honied dews
Of their delight, hung paralyzed with bliss,
 Incapable of motion.

Life's sparkling beaker to the brim was filled,
    Its foamy bubbles, breaking,
    Scattered their fragrant spray,
    Like incense over me.
Oh, God! the quick delight that flashed upon me,
Flooding my spirit with a sea of glory,
Illuminating all its inmost depths
With light's intensity!   Had not my senses
Slept in the death-clasp of a clinging spell
That held them in embraces strong as steel,
This glory had consumed all earthly life.
I floated in an atmosphere of prayer,
Each breath I drew was a sweet inspiration!
Delicious dreamings, visions of delight,
I could have lingered in your beams for ever!

———————

"MY BABY."

Lo, I feel the sweet caresses,
    Of a beauteous angel-child,
Sunny are her golden tresses,
    And her eyes are blue and mild.

Round her flexile mouth, the dimples
    Come and go so sportively,
Changing as the laughing rimples
    When the zephyrs kiss the sea.

On my bosom she reposes,
  Nestling close, she softly sings,
As the rustling of the roses
  From the humming-bird's quick wings.

And a band of angel sisters,
  Smiling, beckoning, hover near,
Lifting her bright head, she whispers
  Kiss me, bless me, mother dear;

Scarce has ceased the pleasant ringing
  Of her voice within mine ear,
When her white arms upward flinging
  Slowly floats she, on, to where

Her companions weave their dances
  On the crimson tinted clouds;
But methinks her parting glances
  An unspoken sadness shroud.

HIDDEN PERFUME.

THEIR choicest odors will the roses keep;
  Their brightest beauties in vailed bosoms cling·
The drowsy minstrels, love-lured, nestle deep,
  Unseen and tuneful in their hearts to sing;
14*

Clothed in a language few can comprehend,
  Their sacred hymnings cunningly they pour,
They best interpret who in reverence bend,
  Learning alone by love's mysterious lore.

Rivers that move with calm and stately motion,
  And lesser streams that bear them company
To the unfathomable depths of ocean,
  Vail half their glories from the common eye.
From lordly oaks that skirt the mountain's brow,
  To the green cedars of the shady vale,
Through each and all, sublimest meanings flow,
  Each hath its lore occult and mystic tale.
And souls of noble strain alone may read
  The lessons folded in their secret core ;
Thus of our souls, heroic thought and deed,
  With reverent love, command the firmest door.

Like a sweet rose-bud doth thy spirit seem,
  Not half its perfume, half its charms revealed;
As the arbutus in dry leaves will gleam,
  Betrayed by incense when the most concealed.
I know that thou art beautiful as bright
  Though but the image of thy soul I see,
For souls like thine disseminate the light
  In glory floods of deep intensity.

VIRGIN ISLAND.

AFAR in the west is a sunny isle
That is only lighted by Woman's smile;
In all its bound may no man be found,
And to woman's voice replies no sound,
But of singing birds, and the minstrelsy
Of swinging boughs in the forests free,—
Of gurgling brooks, and the rippling rills,
And hymns of the flowers on sunny hills,—
And glossy blades of the laughing grass
Kissing our feet as we softly pass,—
And wood-nymphs, borne by the winds above
The Ocean's surges, wooing the love
Of beautiful sylphs, who gambol and play
With the foam-crested waves, or lovingly lay
Their frolicsome heads on the white billows'
    breast,
Whose low, hushing lullaby, soothes them to
    rest.

And O, in this Isle of the Lily and Rose,
All crimson-lipped joys fold their wings in
    repose;
And could I but burst my flesh-fetters I'd soar
On pinions of light to this sweet Island shore,

With gay gladsome spirits to frolic and sing,
Where Winter ne'er darkens our life's joyous
    Spring !

VICTORY.

A STEAMER ploughed Potomac's waves one morn,
    Upon its deck there stood a dark-browed girl
    Like a sultana ; while a haughty curl
Of her proud lip, and a quick glance of scorn,
    Flashing indignant lightning from her eye,
    Told of a purpose resolute and high !
A slave ! this thought within her breast alone
    Came raging ever like an unchecked fire,
    And for fair Freedom such intense desire
Filled her whole being, Reason from its throne
    Fell tottering, as an overwhelming woe
Over her soul in sudden madness came,
And with a shriek that rent the air like flame
    She leapt exultant to the waves below.

SONG OF THE WALKING BEAM SEA ENGINE.

FOR years, long years, down under the wave,
I have toiled, a sullen rebellious slave,
With sad, reluctant, dejected tread,
Not daring to lift my sunken head,
A weary, unwilling subject, bound,
I have plodded on in my ceaseless round.

But now to a broad rejoicing sky,
I toss my fetterless arms on high,
And with head uplifted exultingly,
I shout and I shriek with jubilant glee,
As my mates go by, for I think of the caves,
Far down in the deep, where they toil as slaves.
With a kingly step, stately and proud,
I walk the sea when its waves are loud ;
And I drown with laughter its mocking cries,
When the serried waters around me rise.
Then huzza for the genius that dared to free
From hopeless bondage the King of the Sea.

And huzza for the gallant Captain and crew—
And our ship, that dashes the dark waves
    through,   •

As staunch as iron, as true as steel,
From bowsprit to rudder, from main deck to keel,
And huzza for the Commodore, three times three!
Whose genius has triumphed where science
would flee.

THE ANGEL OF MY DREAM.

I SLEPT as saints may sleep in heaven,
With all their earthly sins forgiven,
And locked within its crystal chains
My soul forgot all mortal pains.

Then I felt a hand on mine,
Seemed it as the touch of thine,
And I straightway turned to see
What thy questioning might be;
'Twas Lucinda's gentle face,
'Twas her sisterly embrace.

Then a curtaining silence fell
And embraced us in its spell,
And her arm was round me thrown,
As a strong protecting zone;
My soul was troubled as a wave,
But her heart beat strong and brave.

" Wherefore, timid spirit, now,
Should'st thou shrink, and tremble so?
Filled with joy thy soul should be,
An angel bends in love o'er thee;
See! he beckons thee away,
Hasten, hasten to obey!"

With a gladsome, sweet surprise,
Lifted I my drooping eyes
Unto his; in either one
Flashed there such a blinding sun,
That beneath their lids in pain,
Mine concealed themselves again.

" Now his glory is more dim,
Thou canst look undaz'd on him."
Lucy said. I looked, and, lo!
Such a rapture lit his brow,
Such a heavenly halo shed
Brightest lustre o'er his head,
That my own I meekly bent,
As a nun before her saint.

Then he took my hand in his,
Oh, of all the memories
That I cherish of the past,
This shall linger, till the last,
O'er my future like a star,
Sorrow cannot dim, nor mar!

"Gentle daughter!" whispered he,
"I am here to comfort thee;
Behold the light about thee shine,
Of my presence 'tis the sign;
When thou feel'st this starry gleam,
Seek me in thy purest dream.

"In deep sorrow, pain, or care,
Or when evil lays its snare,—
In thy every trial hour,
Thou shalt feel the soothing power
My protection can impart,
To support, and cheer thy heart."

Then the darkened heavens bent,
And a fiery cloud was sent,
As the moon appears at times,
When the eastern hill she climbs,
With her garments, crimson red,
O'er the misty orient spread.

Thus intensely luminous
Fell the red cloud over us;
Just above his head it broke,
And involved him in a smoke,
Thin, and clear, and silvery bright,
As a vapor, silvery white.

Round and round him it did twine
Round his matchless form divine,
As a vail of silky gauze ;
And amid the breathless pause
That succeeded our amaze,
Slow he faded from our gaze.

THOU DIDST FORGET.

Thou didst forget to call last night
Upon thy guardian angel bright,
Who hitherto has watched thy sleep,
Its dreaming pure and high to keep ;
Thy nightly prayer thou didst forget,
And with unguarded fancies let
Strange guests into thy spirit come,
Thus driving from their sacred home
The pure and peaceful thoughts serene—
Angels of beauty, who, between
Their heaven and thee, have ever kept
Sweet intercourse ; and, as there swept
Across thy vision, forms so wild,
Sweetly the conscious guardian smiled,
As, with angelic love and grace,
They sought the phantoms to displace.

In thine own soul the power doth lie
To bid each hateful influence fly;
From thine own self the power must come
To lighten and refine thy home;
If thou but speak the magic word
Whereby the soul's deep founts are stirred,
Light, Love, and Truth, will spring to birth,
With the new Heavens and new Earth.

GENIUS OF THE ENCHANTED SPRING.

I HAVE come from stately mountains,
  Where the Indian tribes still dwell;
I have hallowed limpid fountains,
  And blest each crystal well.

O'er bars of steel I've travelled,
  By skilful cunning wrought;
Dark forest paths unravelled,
  With deepest mysteries fraught;

'Mid meads of blooming clover,
  Through sunny valleys fair,
By hill-sides sprinkled over
  With blossoms rich and rare;

Deep, rapid rivers swimming,
  With the Naiads I have strayed;
Where the waves with foam were brimming,
  I have kissed each laughing maid.

Through fields of grain all whitened,
  Ripe for the reaper's hand;
By rippling brooklets brightened
  With sparkling spray and sand;

Where gleaming fish were leaping
  In frolic and in fun;
Where turtles grave were sleeping
  In the smile-warmth of the sun.

By the ever-surging billows
  Of the restless, tireless main;
Where the languid wavelet pillows
  Its head upon the plain.

The clouds have shed a pleasance
  When sunless was my day;
The stars lent their sweet presence
  To gild my nightly way.

O'er the dwellings of the lowly,
  Where truth and love abound,
I have scattered blessings holy
  Of joy and peace around.

Matron and gentle maiden,
　　The youthful and the old,
The gladsome, the grief-laden,
　　Have felt my spirit fold.

And fresh from these caressings
　　Of the lovely and the true,
I come with choicest blessings
　　To shower over you.

Ye are folded to my bosom,
　　Close to my inmost heart,
As the calyx of a blossom
　　Folds in each fragrant part.

CONSOLATION

O DISPEL this wasting anguish,
　　Shed no tears but those of joy,
Lift the falling hands that languish
　　In proud triumph for your boy.

That the golden gates should ope.
　　To his tiny baby feet,
And the words by angels spoken
　　Should his baby spirit greet.

Often in the solemn hushing
  Of the twilight he will steal
So near ye, that the brushing
  Of his pinions, ye shall feel.

To your sad and lonely chamber,
  Seraph babes shall nightly come,
Ye shall hear their pleasant clamor,
  It shall dissipate your gloom.

And upon your loving bosoms,
  On your cheeks and lips so sweet,
Little hands shall lie like blossoms,
  Little lips with kisses meet.

Every eventide the singing
  Of this seraph baby-band,
To your spirits will be bringing
  Echoes from the spirit-land.

————

TO ———

In thy mind, distorted angles
  Here and there obstruct my view;
Reason twisted into tangles,
  Doubt and Trust, the Old and New.
  15*

In thy spirit softly slumbers
   Harmony as rich and deep,
As symphonious in its numbers,
   As o'er heavenly visions sweep.

And a pure and sunny pleasance,
   As a halo seems to rest
O'er thy spirit, and the essence,
   By its sweetness is confest.

In its presence, no denying
   Or foreboding fancies stay,
So the shadows shall be flying
   From thought's song-lit fields away.

Golden gleams shall gild the glooming
   From the sunset's parting glow,
Even the midnight shall be blooming
   Thick with stars upon its brow.

And the glittering dews of sadness
   Shaken from the lap of night,
On the morrow's radiant gladness
   Shall reflect a kindling light.

Light so varied and resplendent
   In its pure and heavenly glow,
It with beauty most transcendent
   Glorifies thy placid brow.

Then, oh then, rejoice for ever,
    That such peacefulness is thine,
There shall come a storm cloud never,
    That can darken o'er the shrine.

THE GARLAND.

I HAVE braided a garland of Asphodel blooms
    Such alone as some magical power enshrine;
Though hueless and viewless, their precious per-
      fumes,
    Will be felt and exhaled by a spirit like thine.

When night wove its webbing of darkness pro-
    found,
    And the zephyrs lay languidly waiting for
      morn,
When the shadows sank silent and slow to the
    ground,
    In a stillness so sacred, the blossoms were
      born.

They were gathered and brought by a seraph to
    me,
    Who said, as she tossed them in the lap of my
      dreams,

"Wake, and weave a wierd wreath ere the in-
        fluence flee,
    And morning dissolve the charmed spell with
        its beams."

So I braided the garland with delicate taste;
    As the last leaf was fastened the bright spirit
        fled;
But in flying she whispered, "In its freshness,
        on, haste!
    Place the magical circlet on sweet Mary's
        head."

THE JEWELED HEAVENS.

On, be silent, spirit voices,
    Singing, ringing, reach my ear,
Throbbing pulses, hush your noises;
    Let me hear! more clearly hear!

Stay, oh stay this tide of feeling;
    Trembling heart, lay fear aside;
Senses, shocked in sudden reeling,
    Look to Him, the Glorified!

Fervently your white arms reaching,
   In the silence lift your prayer,
With lips mute in their beseeching,
   Spirit meekly bending, where

His light footstep flashes beauty
   On the mountains, as he goes;
So the twin eyes, faith and duty,
   To the spirit shall disclose

Such intensely brilliant gleamings
   Of the home where spirits dwell
That the Poet's wildest dreamings
   Were too faint, its worth to tell.

I have seen its mingled glories,
   Flashing intermittent gleams,
Far beyond the gorgeous stories
   Of the heaven of orient dreams!

There the golden chrysoprasus
   Mingled with the emerald's green,
In a glory that surpasses
   All that mortal eye has seen.

The still varying opal's hue,
   The wierd agate's cloudy lines,
Turquoise with its heavenly blue,
   And the flashing almandines.

Diamonds, such as earth ne'er furnished
   For her proudest monarch's crown,
Gems, so exquisitely burnished,
   That their rays like sun-beams shone;

Rubies bright, and pearls the fairest,
   Sea-hued beryls, jasper stones,
And clear crystal forms, the rarest,
   And pellucid chalcedones.

But surpassing all that splendor,
   Blazed the glory of the One,
God-like strong, and child-like tender,
   Whom 'tis life to look upon!

ELYSIAN ECHOES.

WE have read in olden stories,
   How some viewless angel's wing
Could unfold celestial glories,
   Beatific radiance fling
O'er the spirit, when to cheer it,
   Blissful memories it would bring.

We have revelled in the pleasance
   Of some sunny summer's day,

And have trembled in the presence
  Of some glory-bearning ray
From a spirit, when anear it
  God's divinest angels stray.

Golden dreams, which far outnumber
  All the raptures men have sung,
On the silent stream of slumber
  Have as gems of joy been strung
By our visions, when Elysians
  Echoes, through our souls have rung.

And that fountain seems to open,
  So divinely pure and true,
" Who so drinks," thus was it spoken,
  Never more a thirsting knew;
But his spirit should inherit
  Peace, as sweet as heaven's dew.

THE OLD YEAR

Dying, dying, slowly dying,
  Sinks the old year to its rest;
Sighing, sighing, faintly sighing,
  Sleeps the young year on its breast.

Through Time's alcoves sadly ringing
　　Come the songs of angels clear,
Holy anthems, sweetly singing,
　　For the slowly sinking year.

Through the dimly lighted chambers
　　Of the slow receding past,
Gleam the sadly dying embers
　　Of its sacred holocaust.

Now, as voices of the wildwood,
　　Comes a perfect gush of song;
'Tis the gleesome notes of childhood
　　Borne Time's corridors along.

And the Future is unclosing
　　To the young year the "To Be,"
Starting from his sweet reposing
　　Springs he to his destiny.

THE END.

ERRATA.

PAGE 14, 5th line—for *form* read *foam.*

PAGE 176, 9th line—for *on* read *oh.*

Through Time's alcoves sadly ringing
  Come the songs of angels clear,
Holy anthems, sweetly singing,
  For the slowly sinking year.

Through the dimly lighted chambers
  Of the slow receding past,

THE END.